# Nineteen Hundred Days

Florence Osmund

# Acknowledgments

Thank you to the following cast of characters who helped me with this book.

Deborah Bradseth of Tugboat Design—for her creativity on the cover design and attention to detail on the formatting for the paperback, e-book, Kindle, and PDF versions of the book.

Carrie Cantor—not only for her technical editing prowess, but also her invaluable content editing and push to help me become a better writer.

Marge Bousson—for Beta reading this book, providing constructive feedback, and finding those pesky little errors that mysteriously appeared after I had written a flawless manuscript.

Samuel Bishop (14) and Maxwell Bishop (11)—for giving me inspiration and insight into teen and pre-teen boys, so I could get more inside the head of the main character in this book.

# Prologue

This living room holds a curious mix of memories for me—some good, some disheartening, and some I have yet to fully understand. The new memory I will create here today with my daughter Sadie will fall into one of these categories, but into which one, I'm not sure. The discussion I am about to have with her is just the beginning—the memory will need to play itself out.

I still call this Aunt Birdie's house, even though my name is now on the title. With four bedrooms and a big backyard, it suits my growing family. My wife and daughter keep petitioning for a dog, but I haven't yet caved in to that request.

I take a deep breath before I begin the task of reducing a complicated saga—one that consumed my life between the ages of twelve and seventeen—into terms a five-year-old will understand.

"There's something I want to explain to you, Sadie."

"That's okay, Daddy. I don't have to know what you do at work."

"No, sweetie. It's not that." I develop user interfaces for a toy manufacturer. She asked me yesterday what I did at work all day. I explained it to her as best I could, using her LeapPad as an example, but managed to completely lose her. "This is about your grandmother."

"Grandma Tess?"

"No, your other grandma."

"What other grandma?"

"Grandma Tess is your mom's mother. But I have a mother too, and she's your other grandmother. Her name is Grandma Rose."

"I didn't know that."

"I know you didn't."

"So I have two grandmas?" Sadie looks confused but seems to be receptive to the idea. "Where does she live?"

"Well, that's what I want to explain to you. Since before you were born, she's been in, sort of like… She lives far away."

"What's she like, Daddy?"

This is a difficult question for me to answer. I haven't seen my mother in a while, and given where she's been, the years haven't been very kind to her.

"Well, I know one thing," I say to her. "I'll bet she'll be happy to meet her sweet little grandchild for the first time."

"Me?"

She giggles as I tickle her. "Yes, you."

"Why is she coming to see us?"

"Actually, she's going to move here."

"Why?"

As I search for the right words, I am taken back to the day when it all started—the extraordinary chain of events that has for better or worse shaped my life.

Someday, when Sadie is old enough, I'll tell her the whole story. It's one she should know.

# Nineteen Hundred Days

# Chapter 1

It was a Tuesday morning in September of 1998. My dad had just gotten back from driving my mom to work. I was in my sister's bedroom doing schoolwork with her when I heard the phone ring. My dad was in the kitchen, and I could hear snippets of his side of the brief conversation but couldn't make any sense of it. The next thing I knew, he was standing in the doorway of Lucy's room.

"I gotta go. You two squirts behave while I'm gone, ya hear? Your mom needs me for some damn thing or another at what's-her-name's house. Ben, you're in charge. Lucy, do whatever your brother tells you to do." He gave us one of his don't-ask-any-questions looks.

I was twelve and Lucy six.

Every morning, Dad drove Mom to her job, then came home and drank beer until it was time to pick her up. Some days, it was apparent he had stopped somewhere on his way home to have a few. Occasionally, he wouldn't even bother to come home at all after dropping Mom off, and my guess was that he just drank all day at some dive bar until it was time to pick her up. I don't remember him ever going to a job himself.

Mom worked as a caregiver for Mrs. Abigale Washington, a wealthy old lady who lived in Rock Falls, a thirty-minute drive from our house. Mrs. Washington claimed that she was a descendant of George Washington, but Mom had her doubts. Mom described the woman as eccentric, crabby, and demanding, which may have had something to do with her not buying the George Washington connection.

After Dad left for the second time that morning, I got Lucy started on a science project—the life cycle of a butterfly—and then turned my attention to a paper I was writing. We were homeschooled, such as it was. Back then, there didn't appear to be many requirements for homeschooling in our state. Perhaps that's changed by now.

Before work each morning, Mom would give each of us a lesson plan for the day that she pulled from a box she kept in the hall closet. Half the time she was too tired after work to check our work, but I always checked Lucy's. I had once asked Mom why we didn't go to regular school, and she'd given me a vague answer. I later found out from Dad that she'd been relentlessly bullied in school as a child because of her hand-me-down clothes and lack of the same material things the other kids had. She didn't want us to go through the same thing.

On that particular Tuesday, given his history of frequenting bars whenever he had the opportunity, I wasn't too worried when by midday Dad hadn't come home. Lucy and I kept busy most of the day with schoolwork. But when neither of our parents was home by six-thirty—their usual time to get home after Dad picked Mom up from work—I knew something was wrong.

"I'm hungry, Benny," Lucy said. "How long do we have to wait for them?"

I checked the fridge for leftover pizza from the night before, but it was gone.

"A little longer," I told her.

"How much longer?"

"An hour. How's that?"

"I guess," she said as she rolled her eyes.

We watched two episodes of *Family Feud* while we waited. At seven-thirty, I put a package of frozen lasagna in the microwave while Lucy set the table with some of our mismatched plates and silverware.

"Where do you think they are?" she asked.

"I don't know. Sounds like Mom had trouble with Mrs. Washington or something."

"Let's call over there."

"I don't know the number."

We lived halfway between Cattail Creek and Sunfish Slough in a small, ramshackle house we rented in unincorporated Whiteside County, Illinois. Years of neglect from irresponsible tenants had taken a big toll on its condition. All it took was a moderate rain or a few inches of melting snow to flood the backyard and then our storm cellar. That's one of the things I remember most about our house—the dampness. You could feel it on your skin. Mom used to refer to it as clammy. Regardless of the season, it always felt cold and clammy in our house.

An uncommonly long driveway leading up to it made our home invisible from the road, even in winter when foliage on the many spruce and hickory trees that surrounded us was sparse. My parents were somewhat reclusive—the house suited them.

As Lucy and I ate our dinner that night, the aftermath of a slow sunset gradually diminished the scant natural light that came through the kitchen's filmy windows, making our being home alone a bit more foreboding. When we finished eating, we rinsed off the dishes and went into the living room to watch more TV. We had satellite television, but the dish on top of our roof didn't always work right. Unfortunately, this was one of those times. I remember Dad climbing up on the roof to jiggle things connected to the dish until I yelled up to him that we had a picture. At twelve, I wasn't about to climb up on the roof.

"This is boring," Lucy said. "I wish Mom would get home."

"Want me to read you a book?"

"*Pippi Longstocking*?"

She loved those books. I hated them.

"How about the one with the toad and the frog instead?" I offered.

"I want Pippi," she said with conviction.

"Why don't you change into your pajamas first—that way you'll be ready for bed when the time comes."

I retrieved the Pippi book I hated the least, and when Lucy returned in her pajamas, I began reading about the superhumanly strong, red-haired, freckled imp of a girl. By chapter four, when Pippi gets stranded on a deserted island with her pet monkey, Lucy was sound asleep, her head on my lap.

I wouldn't say that Lucy was helpless without me, but she did depend on me. Looking back, I'd say my attention to her needs was more than the average big brother had to give to a little sister.

We had never been left alone overnight before. Sometimes Dad didn't come home after a night of drinking, but Mom had always been there to tuck Lucy into bed and tell me not to stay up too late. I carried Lucy to her room and slipped her into bed without waking her.

The evening dragged. By nine o'clock, there was still no sign of our parents. I thought about calling the police, but I wasn't sure what to tell them without causing a ruckus within my family. Once before, when Dad had had too much to drink and was out of control throwing things and yelling at Mom, I had gotten scared and called 9-1-1. By the time the sheriff arrived, Dad had passed out on the sofa and Mom had cleaned up the mess. After she told him everything was fine, the sheriff eventually left. I got yelled at but good. Mom ended the parental rant by telling me I was lucky Child Protective Services hadn't come and hauled us away. I didn't understand much of what my parents had been fighting about then, but I later deduced it had to do with the fact that my dad wasn't Lucy's biological father, and that was the first he was learning of it.

I tried the TV again and got reception. After watching it for another hour or so—most likely programs I wasn't allowed to watch when my parents were home—I fell asleep on our dilapidated brown-plaid couch—a place where I had taken to sleeping as soon as I'd decided I was too old to be sharing a room with my sister.

# Chapter 2

First thing the next morning, I checked my parents' bedroom, hoping I'd find at least one of them in there, but the still-made bed told me they had not come home. The car wasn't there either, confirming my suspicion. To make sure, I checked the kitchen waste basket for empty beer cans. Finding none on top of the garbage I'd put in there, I knew Dad hadn't been home after I went to bed. Images of caseworkers from Child Protective Services coming to take us away flashed through my mind.

In fact, my biggest fear was of being hauled off by CPS. There was a kid down the street who we'd heard had been snatched from his parents and put into a foster home where he was made to kneel for hours at a time on uncooked rice for punishment whenever he did something wrong. I'd heard of another case in which the foster kid was treated like a second-class citizen in his new home, left behind while the family went on vacations, and forced to sleep on the floor whenever the "real" kids had their friends over for sleepovers. I don't know if any of that was true, but I believed it back then. You believed stuff like that when you're a kid.

I scoured the kitchen for breakfast items. The best I could do was toast with peanut butter, which was pretty hard to swallow without milk. I was choking it down when Lucy came into the kitchen, still in her Little Mermaid pajamas, crying.

"Where *are* they, Benny?" she sobbed. "I want Mom."

My sister—small for her age with long brown hair and big blue eyes—could give off a look that would melt anyone's heart.

"Come here, Luce." I gathered her up in my arms and stroked her moppy hair that was laced with snarls. "Everything will be alright," I said with as much confidence as I could.

She peered up at me, her eyes open wide. "Promise?"

"Yep. Want some toast?"

She nodded.

I told Lucy I was going to search the house for Mrs. Washington's phone number, something I should have done sooner.

"You think Mom's still there?"

"I don't know. But the only way to find out is to call her."

"Can I help you find it?"

"Sure. It'll be like a treasure hunt. You can be Pippi Longstocking."

"Who are you going to be?"

"Um…I'll be her horse."

"That's silly."

"Well, Pippi Longstocking is pretty silly too, so—"

"She is not," she said with her hands planted on her hips.

"Well, her name is silly."

"No, it's not."

"Okay, you're right. But…Philomena Collywobbles is."

Lucy's giggles took my mind off our situation, if only for a few minutes.

After we finished breakfast, we went into our parents' bedroom—the only possible place I could think of to find Mrs. Washington's phone number. When I found a bunch of condoms in the first dresser drawer I opened, I slammed it shut.

"You know what, Luce. Maybe that phone number is in one of the kitchen drawers. Why don't you go check there?"

"But I want to do it with you."

"It'll go faster if we split up."

She left with a sourpuss face, another touching expression of hers that could get to you.

The dresser drawers didn't reveal any kind of paperwork, so I moved on to the closet. Several boxes on the shelf above the hanging clothes caught my attention. I dragged in a kitchen chair and hoisted myself up to reach them.

One box contained a collection of every drawing Lucy and I had ever made. A second one housed lots of papers, but no phone numbers. The last box had been tucked into the far corner, making it difficult to reach. I scooched the chair in and managed to pull the box closer only to find a mess of winter hats, gloves, and scarves. I got down off the chair and checked in on Lucy.

"Find anything?" I asked her.

"I found one of my doll's shoes that I lost a long time ago."

"No phone numbers?"

"Nope. What are we having for lunch?"

"You just had breakfast."

"I know."

I scanned the fridge—one bruised apple, a jar of olives, and several small containers of plain Greek yogurt, the last of which our mother considered a snack. We didn't.

The cupboard proved to be more promising—several cans of soup, chili, and canned vegetables.

"Soup. We can have soup for lunch."

"What kind?"

"Tomato."

Lucy shrugged and left the kitchen. Sometimes it was hard to know what she was thinking. She didn't talk much. I probably hadn't either at her age. Not much opportunity to practice except with each other and Mom and Dad. Where we lived—in the boonies—there were few kids around, and Mom and Dad didn't take us to many places, maybe to Sterling once or twice a year to see a movie or to McDonald's on our birthdays.

A loud rap on our front door caused me to jump up from the chair and hit my knee on the underside of the kitchen table. "Damn!"

No one ever came to our door.

Where was Lucy? I prayed she would remember not to open the door for anyone except family members.

"Lucy," I whispered as loud as I could. "Where are you?"

No answer.

Whoever it was knocked again, this time louder.

"Benny," Lucy shouted.

"Shh!"

To avoid being seen through the living room window, I crawled on my belly through the kitchen and toward Lucy's voice. As soon as I saw her, I motioned for her to go to her bedroom. Still on my belly, I wiggled my way through the hallway before I got up and followed her.

"Who's here?" she asked.

I put my index finger to my lips. "I don't know," I whispered. "Let's wait until they leave."

She seemed scared. I was terrified but tried to appear otherwise. I wanted to peek out the window to see who it was, but I was too petrified.

Whoever was at the front door was now knocking at the back door. My heart thumped hard against my ribs, even more than the time we were home alone and Lucy put her "blankie" too near the burner on the stove where I was boiling water for hot dogs, and it caught fire.

Rooted in place in Lucy's bedroom, my entire body trembling, I remember wondering if anyone in a similar situation had ever had their heart actually explode in their chest and kill them.

I waited for a while before shoving a chair below the high windows to peek out toward the front of the house in time to see our busybody neighbor waddling down our driveway.

"Who was it, Benny?"

"Mrs. Hornblower." The woman's real name was Hanover, but Dad had nicknamed her Hornblower. None of us liked her. I jumped off the chair and faced Lucy. "Until Mom and Dad come home, don't answer the door, no matter who it is. Don't even let them see you inside the house. You got that?"

She looked as though she was about to cry.

"I don't mean to scare you, Luce, but we need to be careful. That's all."

She acknowledged what I'd said with a nod.

"Can you keep busy coloring or something for a while? I've got some thinking to do."

"Where are you going to do that?"

"I'm not sure yet, but I won't leave the house, if that's what you're afraid of."

"Okay."

I went into our parents' bedroom—the only private room in the house besides Lucy's bedroom and the bathroom—and closed the door. My head swirled with questions. How long do we wait for our parents to come home? What happens when we run out of food? What if Mrs. Hornblower comes back?

I went to the kitchen and made a mental list of all the food items in the house. The way I figured it, we could last a week if we rationed them.

If I didn't have to worry about outsiders, Lucy and I could be fine for a week on our own. But that thought brought me back to Mrs. Hornblower. What if she came back with the sheriff or, even worse, CPS? There wasn't a good place to hide if that happened. Or was there?

After peeking out the back window in the kitchen to make sure our neighbor hadn't come back, I slipped out the back door and walked to the storm-cellar door. Seeing it was locked with a padlock, I went back inside.

"Lucy, when you were looking in the kitchen drawers, did you find any keys?"

"One."

"Where?"

"I'll show you."

She retrieved a small key from the silverware drawer. "This one. It goes to the cellar."

"How do you know that?"

"Mom told me."

She'd never told me.

"Are you going in there?" she asked.

"Yeah, why?"

"You don't have to go outside, you know. There's a trap door in Mom and Dad's room."

"There's a what?"

"A trap door. C'mon, I'll show you."

"How do you know this?"

"Mom told me."

Where was I?

Lucy led the way to our parents' closet, lifted up a piece of carpeting that had been glued to a trap door, and pointed.

"There."

I was dumbfounded. I'd lived in this house my whole life and didn't know about the trap door. I put the key in my pocket and stuck my head down the opening. Pitch black and even clammier than the rest of the house.

"Bring me the flashlight, will you?"

"Don't go down there!" she begged.

"Why?"

"I don't want to stay up here all by myself."

That had been a big panic trigger of Lucy's practically her whole life—being left alone—and with Mom working long hours every day and Dad usually half out of it, the burden of making her feel safe usually rested with me.

After I convinced Lucy that I'd be no more than a holler away and for only a minute or two, I climbed down the makeshift ladder into a room no bigger than our bathroom. Empty except for one box, the room didn't seem to be connected to the storm cellar on the other side of the house. I climbed back up the ladder and told Lucy I'd be back in a minute before proceeding outside to the storm-cellar doors. After removing the lock, I eased my way down the ramp to the room the size of a small bedroom with shelving on one wall that held a case of bottled water, a box of protein bars, and Christmas decorations. A few folding chairs leaned up against another wall. I saw no indication that the two rooms were connected.

When I returned, I asked Lucy what else she could tell me about the room in the closet.

She shrugged.

"Do you know why Mom told you about the secret room under their closet?"

"Because I used to be afraid of the bogeyman. She said I'd be safe down there."

"Really."

Her eyes grew wide. "But I think that's where the bogeyman *is*."

"There's no such thing as a bogeyman, you know."

"Mm-hm," she said shaking her head. "Can I go back to coloring now?"

"Go ahead."

I plopped down on Mom and Dad's bed, thinking ahead to what we'd do when we ran out of food, when I remembered our piggy banks. Each birthday and on the occasional holiday, our Aunt Birdie sent each of us a couple of dollars to put in our respective banks. "For a rainy day," she'd always said. I figured if ever there was a "rainy day," this had to be it.

"Hey, Luce! How much money do you have in your piggy bank?"

"I don't know. You can't see much through the crack. Why?"

"Just thinking ahead, that's all."

# Chapter 3

The pounding on the front door jolted me out of a sound sleep, causing me to fall off the sofa and onto the living room floor. After recovering from the fall, I climbed back onto the sofa, stood up on it, and peeked out of the far corner of the high window. A sheriff's car was parked out front.

I ran to Lucy's room. "Get up! Get up!" I whispered as I shook her shoulder. "We're going down to the cellar!"

"What?" she said rubbing her eyes. "Why?"

I plucked her out of bed and dragged her to our parents' bedroom and into the closet.

"Shit! I forgot the flashlight."

"You're going to get into trouble for saying that, Benny."

"Stay here. I'll be right back."

I ran to the kitchen to grab the flashlight, and as I rounded the hallway corner, I lost my balance.

"Damn!"

"I heard you!"

I scooped myself up and stumbled back to the closet, closed the door, and opened the trap door.

"You go down first."

"I'm not going down there," she said.

"You have to, Luce. The sheriff is here. Please…just go down there. Remember, Mom said you'd be safe down there."

She reached for the closet doorknob. "I'm going to get Polly."

Polly was a large dirt-brown dog, her favorite stuffed toy. When she got it for Christmas one year, she asked me to read what was on the tag. "One hundred percent polyester," I told her. Lucy thought that was the dog's name. She shortened it to Polly soon afterward.

I grabbed her hand. "There's no time for that. Now go!"

"I don't want to go down there," she wailed as she slipped down the ladder.

"I'm right behind you, Luce. Don't be scared."

When we reached the bottom, I switched off the flashlight.

"No!" Lucy screamed.

I got on my knees and reached out to hold her. "Look, we can't have the light on," I whispered. "We're safe here. I promise." I sat down on the hard, damp floor. "Here, sit on my lap." I held her and rocked her as I listened to the internal noise of my own fear. I shudder to this day remembering how incapacitated I felt sitting in that dark, damp hole, fearful of what would happen next.

The footsteps and muffled conversation above kept me from saying another word. I identified a male voice and a female one but couldn't make out what they were saying. I rocked a little harder, hoping it would calm Lucy. And myself. The seconds dragged.

"Are they gone?" Lucy asked after a full minute of silence from above. "Can we turn the light back on?"

"Let's wait. I don't want to take any chances."

"How long? I'm cold."

I didn't know how long we should wait before going back upstairs. I thought the quiet might have been a trick.

"How long, Benny? I hate it down here."

"Did you finish your butterfly assignment?" I whispered.

"Yeah. Why?"

"What about the alphabet letters?"

"Mm-hm."

"Even the *Q*? You were having trouble with that one."

"Even the *Q*."

"Good job. Did Mom leave out any more lessons before she left?"

"One, I think, but—"

"We'll check it out tomorrow."

"Benny."

"What, Luce?"

"Why are we hiding from the sheriff? Aren't they our friends?"

"They are...sometimes. Well, here's the thing. Mom and Dad weren't supposed to leave us alone. We're too young. And if the sheriff sees that we're alone, they'll get into trouble, Mom and Dad will, and we'll be put in foster homes."

"What's a foster home? Maybe it's better than being here alone."

Thinking back, she was probably right, but at the time I thought I was the one who knew more about these things.

"Foster homes are where someone gets paid for taking care of you. We don't want that."

"Why not?"

It was hard to explain something that I didn't fully understand myself.

"I heard some of them are really bad. And they could split us up. I won't let that happen."

"Promise?"

"Yep." I hoped it was a promise I could keep.

"Benny."

"What, Luce?"

"I don't want to go to one of those faster homes."

I smiled at her mispronunciation. "I know. Neither do I."

Lucy relaxed in my arms, and after a minute her steady breathing told me she'd fallen asleep.

* * *

I allowed what seemed like an hour to pass before I woke up Lucy. My entire body ached from the awkward position I'd been in, and I had to peel away the damp sweatpants stuck to my bottom and the backs of my legs after I'd been sitting on the wet dirt floor for so long.

"Let me go first," I told her. "I'll check it out and let you know if it's okay for you to come up."

She didn't listen—I could feel her right behind me.

"You're not leaving me down here alone," she said. "I'm coming with you."

"Okay, but be real quiet."

When I reached the top of the ladder, I opened the trap door with my head and saw that the closet door had been left ajar. I listened for noise.

Hearing none, I raised the trap door the rest of the way.

"I think it's safe, Luce."

I waited for her to clear the last step of the ladder before I took her hand and led her into the living room, admitting to myself that holding her hand made me feel a little safer too. I climbed up on the sofa and peered out the window to where the sheriff's car had been parked earlier. The spot was empty.

"It's all good," I said in a normal voice.

"Why do you think they were here?"

"I don't know. But I'll bet Mrs. Hornblower had something to do with it."

"What if they come back?"

"We have our hiding place. We'll be okay," I told her. But I knew in my heart we were in trouble and needed to do something. Just what, I didn't know.

* * *

While Lucy got dressed, I broke into both our piggy banks and counted the money—forty-eight dollars. More than I thought. I wadded it up and stuck it in my pants pocket. Then I got a piece of paper and pencil, drew three columns down the page, and listed our options along with the pros and cons—a decision-making exercise that I remembered from one of my homework assignments.

The first option I considered was to stay put and fend for ourselves until Mom and Dad returned. That way we could stay in familiar surroundings, Mom and Dad wouldn't get into trouble, no one else would have to know our business, and Lucy and I would be together. Lots of pros. Of course, there was the fact that we would eventually run out of money, the sheriff or CPS could find us, and we couldn't leave the house without nosy Mrs. Hornblower seeing us.

Option number two was to get help—turn ourselves in to whoever answered 9-1-1. Then I wouldn't have to handle this all by myself, I wouldn't have to be afraid of what was going to happen to us from day to day, and we'd probably eat better. But they'd likely go after Mom and Dad for leaving us alone, and we could end up in foster homes, possibly two different ones. I didn't think Lucy would do well without me, and I'd be worried sick about her.

And then I had my best idea yet—contact Aunt Birdie. But I didn't know her phone number or the name of the town where she lived. I didn't even know her last name or if Birdie was her real first name or a nickname.

I stared at the list. None of the options was very good. I sat there contemplating our situation before I added another one—venture out on our own and look for a place to stay, a friendly face, someone to look after us until Mom and Dad came home. At least that way Lucy and I would be together. But how would we know whom we could trust not to turn us over to CPS?

I knew deep down that the last idea was stupid, but that didn't stop me from thinking about it.

# Chapter 4

"Lucy, did you find any other keys when you were looking around in the kitchen drawers?" I asked her when she had finished getting dressed and making her bed. I had a wacky idea in my head that wouldn't quit. I knew it to be wrong, and had I been more sensible, I would have stopped thinking about it, but I didn't.

"No, but I know there's a bunch of keys in the breadbox."

"How come you know things about this house that I don't?"

She shrugged. "Maybe because I listen when no one knows I'm there."

I pulled a ring full of keys from the breadbox.

"Do you know what they're for?"

"How would I know that?"

"Just checking. I'm going outside. You stay here. I'll be right back."

"Where are you going?"

"Just outside. You'll be fine."

"I want to go with you."

"No, Luce. I'll only be gone a minute. You can watch me from the window if you want."

My father had a beat-up 1993 white Ford Bronco parked out back that he said would be worth something someday because it was the same make and model vehicle that O.J. Simpson had driven after he'd allegedly killed his ex-wife and her friend. He dusted it off and started it up occasionally but never drove it anywhere.

The musty smell that emanated from inside the car told me he hadn't started it up in some time. I climbed in behind the steering wheel and tried each key in the ignition. When I found the one that fit, I had to scooch way down to reach the foot pedals, preventing me from seeing over the steering wheel. I moved the seat as far up as it would go, put my foot on the gas, and turned the key.

After sputtering a few times, the car's engine turned over. I let it run for a minute before retreating to the house where I contemplated the crazy idea I couldn't let go of—driving away to…I didn't know where.

It wasn't like I'd never driven before—many times Dad had let me switch places with him at the end of our driveway when we came home from running an errand in his other car. I didn't think it was that hard. Of course, that car was much smaller, and I was on private property. Driving the huge Bronco on a regular street with other cars around me would be entirely different.

I checked the ring of keys to see if one fit the back door. I was sure that was how the sheriff had gotten in—Dad had left without locking the door. Not finding a key, I stuck a rubber stop under the door so that if they came back, it would at least slow them down some and give us more time to hide.

Next, I pulled out of the closet the only suitcase I could find—a big, brown trunk-like case that had seen better days—and filled it with things I figured we would need if we were on the run. I wasn't sure at the time why I did this—I may have seen someone do it on TV or something. I threw in some spare clothes, the piggy-bank money, my Swiss Army knife, and a bar of soap. I asked Lucy to put some of her things in there as well. Afterward, when I removed two dolls and her entire set of Pippi Longstocking books, she got mad at me and went to her room to pout. Five minutes later, she was back by my side.

"Are we going to run away?" she asked me in the high-pitched voice she sometimes used when she was upset.

"No."

"Then what's the suitcase for?"

"Just in case."

"In case what?"

"Uh, in case we need to make a quick getaway."

"What's a getaway?"

"Something we may have to do if Mom and Dad don't get home pretty quick."

"Where would we go?"

"Never mind. We probably won't have to do it."

"Are you sure?"

"Yes," I said.

"Okay. Will you play dolls with me?"

"Not right now. Maybe later."

If we did make a quick getaway, I didn't want to leave anything important behind, so I went from room to room searching for things. After collecting two sets of eating utensils, a roll of toilet paper, and a compass, I searched our parents' room.

My dad wasn't a big man—not much taller than I was at the time. Thinking it would be better if I appeared older in case we did have to flee, I took a few of his clothes and laid them out on the bed.

How ignorant I was—thinking of venturing out on my own like I was a grown-up and knew what I was doing. Foolish as it was, my twelve-year-old self was excited at the thought.

* * *

For the second time in as many days, I awoke to someone pounding on the back door. I ran to Lucy's room, shook her awake, and put my hand over her mouth to keep her from saying anything.

"C'mon Luce. You know the drill. Down to the cellar."

Within a few minutes, I was crouched down in the dark, dank room under my parents' closet with Lucy on my lap. This time, she'd had the wherewithal to grab Polly before making the descent.

"I hate this, Benny," Lucy whispered as she clutched the stuffed animal close to her.

"I know. So do I."

"It tastes funny down here."

"I know."

I pushed her hair off her face.

"What did Mom used to do to your hair so it wasn't all in your face like this?"

"I don't know," she said with a shrug. "A barrette maybe."

"We'll have to work on that."

She squirmed in my lap.

"I'm scared," she said.

"I know, but whoever it is will be gone soon."

She shivered. "I'm still scared."

As soon as I felt the warm dampness seep through my pants and onto my skin, I knew what she had done.

"I think I just peed on you, Benny."

"I know. It's okay. We'll wash up after they're gone."

"I want Mom," she said huddling closer to me. "I don't want them to take us away."

"They won't," I said, knowing full well I couldn't be sure about that.

Their muffled voices grew louder—a man's and a woman's. So much for the rubber stopper I'd put at the back door. When the sounds of their footsteps stopped, I feared they were in my parents' bedroom. I motioned to Lucy to be quiet before I slid her off my lap and climbed up the ladder so I could secure the leather strap that hung down from the trap door to ensure the door couldn't be opened by anyone on the other side.

When I was within arm's reach of the strap, the rung I was standing on made a creaking sound. I held my breath. I could make out certain words of their conversation. "Disturbing," he said. "Hospital." "Abandoned."

I secured the strap, crept back down the ladder, and waited.

We heard them leave the room and go somewhere else in the house. Soon after, we heard the front door open and close, leaving behind a dead stillness in the house. After we were pretty sure they were gone, we sat in the silence for at least fifteen more minutes. Then I climbed up into the closet, and when I was certain they had left, I signaled for Lucy to come up too. She was crying.

"Please don't cry, Luce. Everything will be okay," I told her.

"No, it won't," she wailed.

I walked over to her and hugged her. Her whole body felt cold and sweaty.

"How about if I start a bath for you?"

"Can I have bubbles?" she asked through her tears.

"I'll look for some."

Finding no bubble bath, I squirted some dish soap under the running faucet, hoping it would have the same effect.

"Wait!" Lucy shouted. "I forgot Polly down there."

"Okay, calm down. You take your bath. I'll go get her."

The strong smell of urine hit my nose as soon as I opened the trap door. I scampered down the ladder as fast as I could. Once into the room, having forgotten the flashlight, I felt around the floor for Polly when my foot bumped up against the box. It was too heavy to lift, and I wondered what could possibly be inside that weighed so much. I opened the flaps, explored inside with my fingers, and removed a small object—about the size of a TV remote—wrapped in paper. I took it with me upstairs.

While Lucy was still in the bathtub, I unwrapped what I'd found in the box—a carved figure of a man and a lion, the latter pouncing on the former. It appeared to be old and looked like it was made of ivory. I'd never seen anything like it displayed in our home—neither Mom nor Dad was the type to collect things or keep anything around that didn't serve a definite purpose. I went back to the secret room and retrieved as many other items in the box as I could manage in one trip.

"What are you doing?" Lucy asked after picking up Polly and giving the dog a warm hug.

"I found some things down in that room," I told her as I unwrapped the next item. "Whoa!" I rewrapped it so Lucy wouldn't see it—another carved figure, this one of a kneeling woman grabbing on to a man's penis. I had done my share of sneaking peaks at naked people in library books, but never had I seen anything like this.

"What was that?" she asked.

"Nothing. Nothing you'd understand."

"Let me see it."

"It's X-rated. You don't want to see it."

"What's X-rated mean?"

"It means you have to be eighteen to see it."

"You're not eighteen."

"Lucy, believe me, you don't want to see this." I gathered up the individually wrapped parcels and searched for a place to stash them until Lucy went to bed that evening.

"Hey, I think I forgot to close the trap door, Luce. Can you do that for me?"

Lucy stomped off in the direction of our parents' bedroom while I put the parcels in the freezer.

* * *

The day dragged. Lucy and I watched cartoons and played three games of Uno. In between, I made several attempts to do something with her hair, which looked like someone had taken an eggbeater to it. Unfortunately, it was so snarled that when I tried to brush it, she screamed. I didn't know how my mom dealt with it.

Mid-afternoon, it occurred to me that we hadn't checked the mailbox since being home alone. I decided to wait until nighttime to do so to avoid being seen by Mrs. Hornblower.

After playing dolls with Lucy for an agonizing hour, I began the task of preparing dinner.

"Chili again?" she asked.

"It's either that or soup."

"I wish Mom was here. She'd make something way gooder than soup."

"So do I, but she's not, so what do you want for dinner? Chili or soup?"

"Chili. But don't put pepper in it like last night. Too spicy."

After we ate and the sun went down, I slithered my way down to the mailbox, darting between the trees in our front yard and grabbing the handful of mail that had accumulated during the past few days. Once back inside, I separated out the junk mail.

I had to decide whether to open the three pieces of mail that looked important—one from Walter and Edna Fryberg, one from the phone company, and one from American Express. The last two didn't seem like bills, which always came with our name and address showing through the window of the envelope. Instead, our name and address had been typed right onto the envelope.

Considering it preferable to risk getting in trouble for opening my parents' mail than to potentially ignore something important, I opened the letter first.

Dated September 6, the letter was titled FIVE-DAY NOTICE TO QUIT and had an official-looking seal at the bottom. It went on to say that if my parents didn't pay them the $950 they owed in rent within five days of the notice, their lease would be terminated. I turned on the TV to a news channel to find out that day's date—September 10. We had one more day.

A sharp pain struck inside my chest. What did it mean the lease would be "terminated"? I grabbed the beat-up dictionary I used for homework assignments and looked up *terminated.*

    terminate: to bring to an ending or cessation in time, sequence, or continuity.

That definition didn't help me understand the letter. I didn't know if it meant that we had to leave or what would happen if we didn't. Would someone come and drag us out? I wondered if that was why the sheriff had come by.

The letter didn't include the Frybergs' phone number, only their address in Denver, Colorado.

"What did we get?" Lucy asked when she entered the kitchen.

"Nothing much. A lot of junk mail."

"Can I have it?" she asked.

"Sure. Anything in that pile," I told her.

I opened the envelope from the phone company. They said our service was going to be shut off as of September 8 due to non-payment. I picked up our phone. No dial tone. I didn't bother opening the American Express envelope.

After reconsidering the list of options I had jotted down earlier, I realized deep down that I probably should have gone to someone for help right away. I was in over my head.

# Chapter 5

I waited for Lucy to go to bed before bringing up the rest of the items I'd found in the room under the closet. I arranged them on the kitchen table: eight ivory figurines, most of which were of naked men and women; eleven animal figurines carved out of green stone; a gold Hello Kitty figurine with sparkly red, white, and blue stones all over it; a silver purse covered in stones that looked like diamonds to me; a small lamp with a boy leaning against a lamppost; a beat-up letter signed by G. Washington; and a gold locket. I couldn't help staring at the ivory figurines—one was of a fat, naked Asian-looking guy hugging another one from behind. Now, of course, I know what they were doing. At twelve, I had no clue.

I read the G. Washington letter, which was addressed to Lieutenant Colonel Ebenezer Gray and dated November 11, 1782. I didn't understand most of it at the time—something about mutiny, health issues, and more food for the soldiers. I now know our first president was referring to the American Revolutionary War in which he played an important role.

I rewrapped everything and put them into three plastic baggies before shoving them into the suitcase. If we were going to flee, I wasn't about to leave this stuff behind.

* * *

I couldn't sleep that night. All I kept thinking about were the sheriff and CPS coming to get us and forcing Lucy and me to split up and go live with different families. I'd survive, but I knew it would be disastrous for Lucy.

She was just a kid. And she cried a lot. I couldn't let that happen to her.

I was also terrified about what might have happened to Mom and Dad. Neither of them was perfect, but I didn't think they'd have just up and left us to fend for ourselves. Something bad had to have happened to them. It crossed my mind that maybe they were dead, but I tried not to think that could be true. We might not have had the close, loving relationship other children had with their parents, but I still couldn't imagine life without them.

It occurred to me that I could put my dislike of her aside and go next door to Mrs. Hornblower and ask for her help. But that wouldn't keep CPS from taking us away. CPS was the enemy in my mind because why else would Mom and Dad have used them as a threat whenever they were mad at us?

The only way I could see avoiding the enemy was to find Aunt Birdie. We'd been to her house before. Even though I didn't know the name of the town, I thought I could find my way to her house given the opportunity. We always went there the same way—on the road that ran alongside the Mississippi.

I figured our troubles would be over if we could stay with her until Mom and Dad came home. If we only had a way to get there.

Like in the Bronco.

* * *

I waited until midnight before loading up the car with the suitcase, blankets, and pillows, along with a few items of food. I put two of the pillows and a blanket on the driver's seat to prop myself up so I would appear taller and could see over the wheel better.

After donning my dad's jacket and hat, I went in to wake Lucy.

"Come on, little sis. We're going to Aunt Birdie's."

"Huh?"

"Go to the bathroom first."

"What?"

"C'mon. We have to get going."

"Where?"

"Lucy, wake up."

"I'm up. I'm up."

"Go to the bathroom, grab Polly, and let's get going."

"Why are you wearing Dad's coat?"

"Never mind. Just go."

She plodded to the bathroom mumbling something about my not being the boss of her and then took her sweet time doing what she had to do in there. Her dawdling drove me crazy.

"Finally," I said to her. "Do you want to stay in your pj's or get dressed?"

"I'm not going outside in my pj's."

"Okay. Then throw on some clothes, but bring your pj's with."

"Everything's in the suitcase."

"Just wear what you had on yesterday. C'mon, Luce."

She stomped back into her bedroom. When she reemerged, she was wearing a ruffled pink dress Mom had found at the Salvation Army store. The only other time I'd seen her wear it was at a party at Mrs. Washington's a couple of months earlier.

"You can't wear that!"

"Why not?"

"Okay. Fine. Wear that."

Now she was crying.

I heaved a big sigh, walked over to her, and gave her a long hug.

"If we get going right now, we could be at Aunt Birdie's in an hour." I was guessing. I didn't know for sure.

I let go of her as soon as the sobs stopped.

"You okay?"

She nodded, but the scared look on her face told me otherwise.

"You can sleep in the car," I told her. "You and Polly can sleep in the back seat."

* * *

It took me a while to arrange the pillows and blanket just right so I could reach the pedals and see over the steering wheel. When I did, I studied the dashboard to make sure I knew where everything was—headlights, blinker, horn, speedometer, windshield wipers. And gas gauge, which indicated we had a quarter of a tank.

After adjusting the mirrors, to get a feel for it, I started the engine and drove the Bronco down the driveway, headlights off, and then backed it up the drive. Going forward was a lot easier than going backward.

"Where did you say we were going?" Lucy asked.

"Aunt Birdie's."

"All the way up to Momomommies?"

"What are you talking about?"

"Where Aunt Birdie lives. Momomommies."

"Lucy, that makes no sense. Go to sleep."

I reached the bottom of the driveway for the second time and stopped.

"What did you say?" I asked Lucy.

No response.

"Luce!"

"You told me to go to sleep."

"Were you trying to pronounce the name of her town, where Aunt Birdie lives?"

"Yeah."

"How do you know what town she lives in?"

"Dad told me."

I backed the car up the driveway for the second time and checked the glove compartment for a map.

I wasn't good at reading maps. I was reminded of one time I was in the car with my dad and he asked me to look at the map and tell me if he had passed a certain road. I couldn't do it. He got mad and had to pull over to read it himself. This time wasn't any easier.

I did manage to find the Mississippi River on the map and traced my finger along it until I spotted Fulton, a town not too far from us. I continued running my finger up the page until I found a town that sounded somewhat like what Lucy had said, close to the Wisconsin border. Menominee was straight up the river, which was where I was pretty sure Aunt Birdie lived. That had to be it. At least now I had a town.

"You're alright, Luce," I said as I folded up the map. When I got no response, I restarted the car, drove down the driveway for the third time, flipped on the headlights, and turned left.

The clock in the car said two a.m. I didn't remember it ever taking any longer than an hour to get to Aunt Birdie's, but I had never really paid close attention to the time. Before making this decision to drive, I hadn't considered the consequences of arriving at my aunt's house at three in the morning—but now I figured that if we had to, we'd wait in the car until we saw lights go on in her house.

With no other cars in sight, pulling out onto the road was easy. I knew the way to Walter Road, and I was almost one hundred percent sure that was the road we took to Aunt Birdie's. I remember the night sky being very clear, the air still, and the atmosphere eerily quiet.

The first stop sign scared me a little because another car was stopped at the intersection when I arrived. I slowed down so that the driver would know to go first, and when I got close, I glanced down so as not to show my twelve-year-old face. It was only when I came to a complete stop that I had the wherewithal to loosen the death grip I had on the steering wheel.

At the next stop sign, when I went to brake, my foot slipped off the pedal, causing me to lunge forward and hit my mouth on the steering wheel. I lost control of the car for a few seconds before I found the brake again, and when I did, I had to back off the curb that I had run over to get back on track. Fortunately, no one else was around to witness my missteps.

Walter Road, a two-lane major road that ran alongside the Mississippi for miles, was quiet, and I was able to turn onto it without incident. The first mile or so was a breeze—farms everywhere, no traffic, not even a stop sign. The 35-mph speed limit was easy to maintain. I felt good behind the wheel. Grown-up. I puffed my chest out a little, gloating a bit.

When I reached Fulton, things changed—still farms on the left but single-family homes on the right with cross street after cross street to consider for cars coming out. Torn between keeping my eye on the road in front of me and watching for other cars, I soon became so nervous that I felt the need to pull over to compose myself.

The road curved, and now homes lined both sides of the road, twice as many places for cars to dart out at me. Afraid the pressure in my chest was going to squeeze all the air out of my lungs, I turned right at the next side street, which dead-ended at the edge of someone's farm. I threw the car in park, unsnapped my seatbelt, and got out.

It felt good to walk around a bit. I checked on Lucy, who was still asleep in the back seat, then retrieved a bottle of water and gulped down half of it.

Feeling a bit calmer, I got back into the Bronco and attempted to turn it around. Several minutes later, I had the car facing the right direction and, despite the new anxiety that the turning-around maneuver had caused, continued on my way.

After a short while, the scenery changed back to farmland, making the drive easier. I drove for several more miles without seeing another car on the road. When I approached the first stop sign in miles and applied the brake, a loud thumping noise resounded from somewhere under the vehicle, toward the back. When I brought the car to a stop, the noise disappeared.

I didn't know whether to stay put or move on.

# Chapter 6

Hands frozen on the steering wheel, I let my foot off the brake and placed it on the gas pedal. The car noise started out mild but grew thunderous within seconds.

"What's that banging noise?" Lucy shouted from the back seat.

"I don't know, Luce. I'm going to pull over and see if I can see anything underneath." I managed to stay calm for her when what I really wanted to do was scream.

I turned onto the next street and into the parking lot of Casey's General Store, coasting past the gas pumps to the far edge of the lot toward the back of the store and stopping near a lamppost. While I didn't know what to look for underneath the car, I was relieved when I didn't see anything dangling. Finding no flashlight in the glove compartment, I walked around to the back of the vehicle to check for anything suspicious, thinking maybe I'd run over something. The hazy gray sky and stillness in the air creeped me out—the slightest noise making me cringe. No other people were in sight, and at the time, I wasn't sure if that should have been comforting or added to my fears. I squatted down to peer under the car but saw nothing unusual, so I stood up to think through my next move.

A man standing in the shadows of the building smoking a cigarette caught my attention, but he didn't appear to be paying us any mind, so I tried to ignore his presence by continuing with the mission at hand. When I lifted the tailgate to make sure it had been properly closed, I noticed Lucy rummaging through the suitcase.

"Hey, what's this?" she asked holding up the Hello Kitty figurine.

"Put that back!" I said forcefully enough for her to know I meant business but not loud enough for the man in the shadows to hear. "It's not a toy."

"It looks like one."

"Lucy, put it back in the suitcase. Now!"

About to cry, Lucy slipped the figurine back into the suitcase and slumped back into her seat.

"Do you need any help?"

The voice, while soft-spoken, startled me. In my haste to duck out of the back of the car, I hit my head.

"You okay, kid?" It was the man with the cigarette. His disheveled clothing made me back away.

"Yeah, sure. We just stopped here for a bit. Nothing wrong."

"Yes, there is," Lucy chimed in. "Our car is making a funny noise."

He peered into the back seat and gave Lucy a long glance. "Nice dress, sweetie."

"What kind of noise?" he asked me, not taking his eyes off Lucy. "Maybe I can help you. I know a little about cars."

I kept my head down so he wouldn't get a good look at my face.

"It's nothing really. We're going to be on our way."

The man grabbed my arm. "Hey, how old are you?"

"Sixteen," I said, barely getting the word out.

"You don't look sixteen."

"I know. I get that all the time," I told him through a whimper.

"Do you have a driver's license?"

I didn't respond.

"Look, you seem to be in a bit of trouble here. Let me help you."

He sounded okay, but I couldn't tell much by observing him from the waist down. After a few agonizingly long seconds, I mustered the courage to look him in the eye.

He was scrawny, younger than I expected—around the same age as my parents—with long dark hair gathered in a messy ponytail. My eyes were drawn to the tattoos on his arms, including one that said CELL WARRIOR.

The man tugged at his shirt sleeve. "Pay no mind to those."

Not knowing where to look or what to say, I stood there like the dumb twelve-year-old that I was until I became frozen in both speech and stance.

"Why don't you hand me the keys, kid, and I'll see if I can tell what's wrong."

A warning bell rang in my head, but not loud enough for me to get the hell out of there.

"No, I'll start it up."

I got behind the wheel, started the engine, and didn't do anything for several seconds while I contemplated whether to speed away from this guy or let him help us. That's when I noticed Lucy had gotten out of the car to talk to him. I rolled down the window.

"Lucy, stay in the car."

"Why?"

"Because I said so."

"Melvin said we could come back to his house if we want," she said standing next to him. "He says he may have some candy there."

"Get back in the car."

Everything felt wrong—I'd watched enough episodes of *Unsolved Mysteries* to know we could potentially be in big trouble.

After Lucy got back in the car, I drove away, still not sure what I was going to do. The thumping noise was louder than ever.

"Stop!" the man yelled and rushed over to my open window.

"I wouldn't drive it, son. It could be anything, but if it's the brakes, you don't want to take any chances." He leaned in my window, the gold cross he wore around his neck dangling outside of his shirt, the stench of cigarettes cascading off his tongue. "I suggest you park the car, lock it up, and come home with me. This is no place for a couple of kids to be hanging out. I'll call someone for you when normal people are up. You got insurance on this thing?"

I shrugged.

"Family? You got a family member I could call?"

"Nope."

"You two are out here at three in the morning all by yourselves."

"Yep."

"With no driver's license."

I didn't respond.

"Best come with me, because if you don't, well, I'll have to call the police. Because you shouldn't be out on the road. And I'd hate to see what happens to you then."

I knew we'd be in trouble for sure if the police were called. Then CPS.

"Okay," I told him.

After I parked the car, I made sure everything I needed was in the suitcase and then locked the car.

"When's the last time you ate?" he asked. "They serve breakfast all night in here."

"We're okay," I told him.

"I'm hungry," Lucy said.

"We're fine. We already had breakfast."

"I didn't," Lucy clarified.

I scowled at her, a gesture I'm sure she didn't understand. When I turned toward the man, he was heading toward the general store.

He turned to us. "So is it breakfast or not?" he asked.

I met Lucy's gaze.

"We're good," I said.

"C'mon in, then. I'll pick up some sandwiches," he said.

We followed him to the refrigerated section of the store where he picked up six sandwiches.

"You like ham?" he asked.

We both nodded. Either three more people at his home were expecting sandwiches or he was planning ahead for us. Both scenarios scared me.

It crossed my mind to run over to someone else in the store and ask for help, but I didn't want to make a fool of myself. And as I saw it, this guy was going to help us avoid the police and CPS.

He paid for the food, and we proceeded to leave the store.

"Wait a minute," I said. "How's the car going to get fixed if I still have the key?" I asked. "Maybe we should wait here."

"No one is going to fix it here. I'll have to call a tow truck. They can tow it without a key."

"How much will that cost?" I asked.

"I know someone. Don't worry about it, kid."

He headed out the door toward his vehicle—a beat-up red pickup truck. The cool night air felt both refreshing on my face and chilling at the same time. All I could think of was the numerous times we'd been told to never get into a car with a stranger, and I had to remind myself that even though he appeared to want to help us, Melvin was still a stranger.

In a fit of panic, I grabbed Lucy's arm and pulled her in the direction of the general store. I hadn't gotten far when Melvin grabbed my other arm, the one dragging the suitcase. His grip lasted a mere few seconds before he spun me around and then let go.

"Look, kid, you can run into that store for someone else to help you. I'm not going to stop you—no skin off my nose. But they're going to do one of two things to you—turn you over to the police or bring you back home. Now, I'm assuming you don't want to go back home, otherwise you wouldn't have left there. So that leaves the police…and you've been driving without a license. Right? They'll take you in for that, and then what happens to your pretty little sister here? Like I said, the choice is yours. I've got better things to do with my time than to help a couple of snot-nosed kids who don't even appreciate it."

He turned his back on us and headed toward his truck.

"I don't want to go to a lobster home, Benny!" Lucy wailed.

# Chapter 7

The decision to go with Melvin or try to get help from someone inside Casey's General Store didn't come easily that day. I was pretty sure Melvin was right—that if we went inside and asked for help, the police would be there in no time, and that meant CPS would be involved if they couldn't locate our parents. At least with Melvin, it seemed like we could avoid that, and my pathetically innocent mind figured if his intention was to hurt us, he wouldn't have walked away like that.

"Hey, Melvin. Dude!" I shouted at him.

He turned around to face us.

"Can I ask you something?"

"Shoot."

"Why do you want to help us?"

He walked back toward where we stood.

"Because I know what it's like to be alone, scared." He shifted his weight. "Look, when I was a kid, my father walked out. My mother was too drunk to do any kid-raising. Being the oldest, I had to make the decisions. It's no fun. I've been there. Been in your shoes. But, like I said, the choice is yours."

Lucy, who had wrapped her arms around my waist, tightened her grip.

"I don't want us to be split up," I told him.

"I hear ya," he said before he retreated to his truck.

"I'm tired, Benny."

We walked to his vehicle.

"You can put the suitcase in the back," he said without looking at me.

"It won't fly out?" I asked.

"I'll drive slow. It'll be fine."

I deposited the suitcase in the bed of his truck, knowing full well that going with him was not the right thing to do but feeling like I had little choice. After Lucy and I climbed into the front seat, she tucked her head under my arm and held on to me like she was about to go on a roller coaster ride.

"How far from here do you live?" I asked.

"Not far."

* * *

I felt sick with terror during the ride with Melvin. After driving for twenty minutes or so, he pulled into the long, dark driveway of someone's farm. When he drove past the farmhouse down an endless dirt road to the back of the property, my feeling of dread worsened.

Due to the pitch-blackness of the area and Melvin's truck having only one headlight, I didn't see the small mobile home until we were right in front of it. He parked just outside the gate of a chain-link fence that surrounded the home. Before he exited the truck, he pushed a button on a remote control clipped onto the visor, which activated a spotlight that hung over one of the doors of the home.

"Gets fuckin' dark out here in the middle of nowhere," he said.

As we walked to the dwelling, I could see bits of gray paint showing through large patches of rust along the front. Several broken cement blocks served as steps up to one of the two doors, leaving the other door difficult to reach even for someone with long legs.

"Why are there two doors?" I asked him as he opened the gate to the chain-link fence.

"Damned if I know. One goes into the living room and the other the bedroom. Stupid trailer came that way."

We followed him inside.

Except for the bathroom and bedroom, the entire home was one room. And I had thought my family's house was small. Rumpled clothes were strewn around. More clothes hung from the curtain rods—whether to provide privacy or to drip dry I wasn't sure. Dirty dishes covered the scant kitchen-counter space, and a yellow bug-strip hung down from one of the ceiling panels over the stove. At least our house didn't smell.

"Take a load off," he said. "You can put the suitcase over there," he said gesturing to the small space between a badly stained sofa—the only free-standing item of furniture in the room besides the coffee table—and a built-in corner booth where a maximum of three people could eat. He snatched a girlie magazine off the coffee table and threw it into the bedroom. "Real chicks are nothing but trouble," he said looking directly at Lucy.

"I'm tired," Lucy said. I didn't know the time, but because the sun hadn't come up yet, I knew it was still pretty early.

I reached into the suitcase, pulled out a blanket and pillow, and after checking to make sure the bench seat of the small booth was relatively clean, arranged the bedding for Lucy.

"Here, Luce. Try to go back to sleep."

"Where will you be?" she asked.

"Right here. On the sofa."

"Can I have Polly?"

I pulled out the stuffed dog and handed it to her.

Melvin put the sandwiches he'd bought into the countertop fridge, retrieved a beer, and joined me on the sofa.

"You don't mind if I have a cold one, do you?"

Mind? It was his house.

I shook my head.

"Want one?"

I shook my head harder.

"I'll call my buddy Dick after nine." He laughed. "He'd have my ass if I called him this early."

"Okay."

"He can tow your car here, and we'll take a look at it."

"Okay."

"You gonna tell me why you and your sister are running away?"

I didn't look at his face, couldn't. I shrugged, not knowing how to answer the question.

"If I knew, maybe I could help you more."

That made sense, but still I hesitated to tell him too much of our business.

"Where are your parents?"

"They're around."

"You don't know where they are?"

"Not really."

"So why'd you leave home?"

"We're on our way to live with our aunt."

"I see. Does she know you're coming?"

I shook my head.

"Where does she live?"

"Not far from here."

"What town?"

"I don't know how to pronounce it. Momomommies."

"Menominee?"

"Yeah, that's it."

"Well, you're close. It's about ten miles north of here. Where'd you come from?"

"Near Fulton."

He raised his voice. "You drove all the way here from Fulton?"

"Mm-hm."

"You drove here, clear from Fulton, in the middle of the night, with no driver's license." He held up his free hand for a high-five. "That's got to be forty miles. Not bad, you little shit. You ever drive before?"

The conversation made me feel better about being there, a little more relaxed. "Just up and down our driveway," I told him. "It's a long driveway."

He got up and turned on the TV.

"I don't get good reception here, but maybe something is on."

Finding an episode of *The Simpsons,* he turned up the volume and rejoined me on the sofa.

"Ever watch this?"

"Sure."

"Bet you don't get half the jokes. I wouldn't have when I was your age."

We watched in silence for a few minutes. I couldn't concentrate on the show.

As much as I tried not to think of it, I had to go to the bathroom…bad. But I didn't want to leave the suitcase and Lucy alone with him. He must have noticed my squirming.

"Feel free to use the can if you need to," he said. "It might be relatively clean."

"Yeah, I will."

"You can trust me, you know."

"Mm-hm," I said, my eyes glued to the TV.

"I may appear to be nothing more than a good-for-nothing son-of-a-bitch, but I ain't gonna do you no harm."

I didn't know how to respond to that.

"You and me, we may be a lot alike, kid. On your own. Damned, no matter what you do. Know what I mean?"

"Not really."

"You can't go home, can you?"

I shrugged.

"If you could, you'd be there. Right?"

"I guess so."

"Can't go to the police either? Right?"

I shook my head.

"'Cause of what's in the suitcase?"

"No." I didn't like where this conversation was going.

"Why then?"

"They'll call CPS."

"Hey, that might not be so bad. Three hots and a cot every day. Roof over your head. What's wrong with that?"

"They'd split us up, and I'm not going to let that happen," I blurted out.

"Okay. Calm down, bud."

"I'm hungry," Lucy said as she sat up from her sleeping position on the bench seat, "and sore."

"Come here, little girl," he said. "I'll rub your shoulders."

"I'll do it!" I said.

"I have to go to the bathroom," she whispered.

"Come on, then," I said as I rose from the couch.

She gave me a puzzled look. "I can go by myself, you know."

After I gave the bathroom a once-over, I closed the door after her, and when she finished and came back out, I gave her a gentle push back into the bathroom.

"What are you doing?"

"Turn around," I whispered.

"Why?"

"Just because. Keep your back to me while I go."

"This is weird, Benny."

I didn't care what she thought at that moment.

When we got back, Melvin said, "I called Dick, who's real pissed I woke him. He can't pick up the car until tomorrow. His sister's wedding is today, and he's got things to do."

"Why can't we just call a towing company?"

"You got a hundred bucks?"

"No."

"Well, neither do I, and the Dickmeister won't charge us."

"Oh."

"You can stay here 'til tomorrow," he said through a slight smile.

# Chapter 8

Melvin's words—which he had spoken in a calm voice—echoed in my head for the longest time. "You can stay here 'til tomorrow," he'd said. A whole day and night with him.

I kept thinking Lucy and I should simply bolt and get away from this man. But where would we go? The dirt road leading to his mobile home had been long—we'd never make it out without him catching up to us if he wanted. But the thought of spending so much time with him left a queasy feeling in my stomach.

"Are you still hungry, darlin'?" he asked Lucy.

She didn't respond, and the frightened look on her face made me feel that much worse.

"It's kind of early for those sandwiches, but you can have one if you like. Or half of one. Whatever you want." He laughed a peculiar laugh. "Pretty, but not very talkative, is she?" he said to me.

"No, she's not," I said with conviction.

"Calm down, kid. I didn't mean anything by it." When he got up to retrieve the sandwich, I had to wipe away the sweat that had dripped down the side of my face despite it not being warm in the room.

"You want one, buddy?" he asked.

"No, thanks. I'll wait." I couldn't eat.

After he served Lucy her sandwich on top of the bag it had come in, he settled back down on the sofa.

"You mentioned CPS. You're right to try to avoid them—they're nothing but a bunch of overpaid transporters, moving you from one bad house to another. You know anyone who's ever been in a foster home?"

"Yeah."

"Good experience?"

"Nope."

He slouched down into the sofa. "Dated this chick once. Well, not really. Never took her anywhere. Hung out here mostly. She lived in foster homes practically her whole life. All hell-holes—worse than the real one she was ripped out of. Her caseworker told her that putting her in a foster home was to punish her parents for not taking care of her. But she thought just the opposite—that it was punishment for her." He smiled. "Nice girl. Nice, but royally fucked up."

He shook his head and continued talking, almost to himself now. "At least I didn't have to go through that as a kid, though I'm not sure why we didn't get taken away from our whore of a mother." He stared into space for a few seconds before turning to me. "You think you had it bad? When I was your age, seven of us lived in this two-bedroom pigsty in a neighborhood not fit for the rats that roamed the streets at night. No heat in the winter. Electricity turned off every other month." He took the last swig of beer from the can. "A drunk of a mother who was more interested in the stupid men in her life than she was raising us kids. No wonder I drink."

I didn't know what to say, so I said nothing.

"Bastard father walked out on us right after Jimmy was born." He smashed the beer can on the arm of the sofa. "If I knew where that son-of-a-bitch was, I'd probably kill him."

I tried to swallow my spit, but I didn't have enough to swallow. The guttural noise I made in the process caused Melvin to react.

"You okay, kid?"

"I'd like some water, please."

"I ain't got none of that fancy bottled stuff. All I have is right out of the tap. Well water. It ain't bad."

"That's fine."

"There may be a plastic cup in that cupboard," he said pointing in the general direction of the kitchen area.

I had never tasted well water before—it was hard getting past the putrid smell. I drank enough to coat my dry throat.

"If it tastes a little funny, it's because sometimes the septic line leaks into the well. That's why I drink beer." He paused. "Well, not the only reason."

At the time, I didn't know what a septic line was. Now, I'm glad I didn't.

"Hey, wanna hear a joke?"

It had been my experience that adults never told funny jokes. Or maybe they were funny, but I just didn't get them. I thought maybe Melvin would be different.

"Sure."

"What do you do when your dishwasher stops working?"

"I give up."

"Slap her on the ass and tell her to get back to work."

He burst out laughing, banging his fist on his leg several times.

"How is a girlfriend like a laxative?"

I shook my head.

"They both irritate the shit out of you."

He was great at laughing at his own jokes.

"Okay, one more. What do you call someone who refuses to fart in public?"

"Polite?"

"No. A private tutor."

I had to admit the last one was pretty funny. At least it was one I could repeat.

"I got a million of 'em."

I glanced at Lucy, happy to see she was busy eating her sandwich and paying more attention to Polly than to us. When she finished, I told her to put the paper bag on the kitchen counter and go wash her hands.

"Cute kid," he said eyeing his watch. "So here's the deal. It's eight o'clock. I've got an AA meeting at nine—one of my sister's many stupid conditions for my staying here. All I have to do is show up. Won't take me long. You guys okay by yourself?"

"Sure," I said, thoughts about how to escape already forming in my head.

"You won't try anything stupid now, will you?"

I shook my head. "Can we watch TV while you're gone?"

"Hell if I care. Watch whatever you want, but nothing in the 500s, unless you're into porn."

"Okay," I told him, like that was even an issue.

He wolfed down a sandwich and another beer before leaving.

"I'm blowing out of here. See you in a bit."

It wasn't until the sound of his truck faded into the distance that I was able to breathe easily again.

"He's weird," Lucy said.

"Yeah, well, don't tell *him* that."

"I'm not stupid, Benny."

I decided to check our suitcase to make sure everything was intact. It hadn't been out of my sight except for when I went to the bathroom, but I didn't think I could trust this guy, not all the way. The suitcase was still exactly where I'd placed it—on the floor under the tabletop of the booth where Lucy had slept, covering up missing linoleum tiles—except now the handle was handcuffed to the leg of the table. I bent down to get a closer look and then tried to lift the table leg to free the handcuffs—it wouldn't budge. Apparently, he wanted to make sure we didn't leave. That contradicted his comment back in Casey's parking lot where he'd told us he wouldn't stop us if we wanted to leave.

"When are we going to Aunt Birdie's?" Lucy asked.

"Soon, Luce."

"Today?"

"No, not today. We have to wait for our car to get fixed."

"Are you going to drive it again?"

"Maybe."

"I don't think you should. Melvin said the police could arrest you."

"They won't."

"Are we going to stay here until we get the car?"

I glanced at the handcuffed suitcase. "Looks like we don't have much choice."

"I don't like it here. It smells funny."

"I know, but it won't be long. As soon as the car is fixed, we're out of here," I said, feigning more confidence than I actually felt.

"Do you think he gets *Care Bears* on his TV?" she asked.

"I'll check."

* * *

Melvin returned within the hour, swearing up a storm about having to hang out with those "goddamn program people."

"Nothing but a bunch of arrogant alkies, that's all they are. And don't even get me started on my Big Book–thumping sponsor," he said as he cracked open another can of beer. "Assholes."

We didn't say a word. He reminded me of our mother—an easy-going person most of the time, but someone who let things build up inside of her until they hit a boiling point before she'd snap. Our dad had been good at predicting when she was about to explode and could usually stop it from happening. At that moment, I was wishing I'd paid closer attention to how he did that.

"You really like this shit?" he asked about the TV show we had been watching.

"She does," I said.

He flipped through the channels until he reached something he liked. "Here—this is better."

We sat in silence through three episodes of *Cops*. Melvin dozed off periodically, snoring up a storm, but somehow still managed to hang on to the beer can in his right hand. Lucy sat close to me and hid her face in my armpit during scenes that contained blood, violence, and swearing.

"When I was a kid, I thought I wanted to be a cop when I grew up," Melvin said during one of his conscious periods. "Ha! Like that was ever going to happen. You need at least a high school diploma to be a cop—I couldn't even manage that. You like school, kid?"

"It's okay."

"Waste of time, if you ask me. I could have a PhD, which stands for 'piled higher and deeper,' in case you didn't know, and I'd still be doin' what I'm doin' for work."

"What do you do?"

"I flip burgers at Florrie's three days a week. Just enough to live on and keep Nurse Ratched off my back. It sucks, like any job, but I get free food, so I guess I can't complain. If I did, no one would listen anyway."

"Nurse Ratched?"

"My sister. Her real name is Rachael, but I call her Nurse Ratched. Ever see *One Flew Over the Cuckoo's Nest*?"

"No."

"You should someday. A real classic. My sister is a nurse. Lives in the big house with her three bratty kids and a flea-ridden mutt of a dog who lovingly shows his teeth whenever he sees me. Dog ought to be shot."

Despite everything else he said, I found it comforting to learn that a mom lived in the farmhouse.

"She got me a job at the hospital once, in the maintenance department.

Lasted about a week. Less maybe. Working full-time is for chumps. What does your old man do?"

"He doesn't work."

"Your mom?"

"She takes care of a rich lady."

"See? Your old man's got it right! Good for him."

The day dragged. Unlike Melvin, I could only stand to watch so many episodes of *Cops*. Lucy took two naps. I spent my time thinking about how I would manage to guard Lucy and the suitcase and still manage to get some sleep when night fell.

# Chapter 9

I awoke to a deafening noise—a constant rhythmic hammering on the roof—and something wet dripping on my face. My automatic response was to roll off the couch, after which I landed on the floor on my hands and knees. Now fully awake, I wrapped my arms around my head for protection.

"Benny!" Lucy shouted. "What's going on? I'm scared!"

I lifted my head and, still on my hands and knees, followed her voice through the pitch-dark room until I found her huddled in the corner of the bench in the dining booth.

"Stay there, Luce. I'll try to find the light switch."

I fingered my way around the perimeter of the room until I touched a switch, only to find it non-functioning.

"I'm afraid, Benny," she cried. "What's all that pounding?"

"Hold on a minute." As soon as I said that, a loud clap of thunder rumbled through the place, followed by lightning that lit up the room. The rain battered the roof with such force that it veritably shook the mobile home.

"It's raining on my head, Benny!"

"Goddamn rain," Melvin said as he emerged from his bedroom. "Why don't you turn on some lights?" he shouted.

"I tried that switch over there, but it doesn't work," I told him.

"Stupid generator must have gone out. Or run out of gas. Always something." He stumbled his way to the kitchen area and came back with several buckets and a lantern, which he put on the dining table. The scant light from the lantern allowed me to see what Melvin was wearing—only his boxer shorts.

Lucy was crouching in the corner of the bench seat with her hands on top of her head.

Melvin slid a bucket on the table toward her. "Here, darlin'. Put this where you're sitting and come out of there. Damn roof leaks like a sieve." He handed another bucket to me. "Put this one on the couch where it's coming in." He picked up the other buckets and placed them in various spots to catch the rain.

The downpour, propelled by a blustery wind, continued to violate the roof with such vengeance, I expected it to fly off at any moment.

"Does this happen often?" I asked.

"This hard of a rain, you mean?"

"That, and the lights not working."

"Few times a year, I guess. Keep your eye on the buckets and dump them in the sink when they get full. I'm going to check the generator 'round back."

Lucy ran over to me as soon as Melvin left and grabbed me around my waist. "I want to go home," she wailed.

"We can't," I told her as I stroked the top of her head. "Not just yet." I took her gently by the shoulders and looked her straight in the eye. "Did you sleep okay last night?"

"Mm-hm."

"You didn't wake up at all? Nobody woke you up?"

"The rain woke me up."

A wave of relief surged through my body knowing Lucy had been untouched throughout the night, relieving me of the guilt I felt for falling asleep. I picked up the suitcase and rifled through it, reasonably assured that it had remained untouched as well.

"What are you looking for?" Melvin's voice startled me.

"Nothing. Just checking our clothes."

"And what did you find?"

"They're still here," I said, realizing as soon as I said it that it was a stupid response.

"Where'd you think they'd be?"

I shrugged, hoping he remembered that I was just a dumb kid who sometimes said and did dumb things.

"Mm-hm. So when are you going to tell me about—" His ringing phone interrupted his question. "I don't know," he said into the phone. "Haven't checked it out yet. It's raining too fucking hard for me to go out there. My guess is it'll be under water for a few days." He puffed on a cigarette while the other person spoke. "Sounds like a plan," he said before clicking off the phone.

"That was Dick, asking if the road up here is drivable. I doubt it, especially for his tow truck. He's going to check out your Bronco in the parking lot as soon as it gets light out and see what he can do."

"How will he get into it? It's locked."

"He's got tools." He squished out his cigarette in the sink. "I've got some cereal in the cupboard. You kids want some breakfast?"

We both nodded.

"Check the cupboard over the microwave, the one with the missing door. Milk is in the fridge."

"Bowls?" I asked.

"The other cupboard."

I found two spoons on my own and set up our breakfast at the table.

"Ha! I've lived here for over two years and never once eaten at that table," he said. "'Course I eat out most of—"

A loud rap on the door cut him off.

"Shit. That can only be one person—Nurse Ratched."

He sauntered over to the door, mumbling something inaudible before opening it.

The woman came in with her head down, presumably shielding her face from the driving rain. Streams of water ran off her yellow slicker as she stood a few feet in front of the still-open door.

"Step in more," Melvin snapped. "Geez, Rachael, you're making a mess in here."

"It's about time this floor saw some water," she said as she shook herself off. "Add a little soap, and it would get a washing for the first time since you've lived here."

"Put a sock in it, Nurse Ratched. Here, gimme your coat."

"Put some clothes on, you fool," she told him. "You always walk around in your underwear?"

She was short—not much taller than I was—and tiny, reminding me of our mother. When she finally noticed Lucy and me, she didn't say anything—just stared at us with her mouth open. When she finally spoke, the words had a hard time coming out.

"What the hell— Who's this?" she asked.

"This is Ben and his sister, Lucy."

"What…what are they doing? What are they doing *here*?"

"Calm down, sis. I'm just helping them with their car. That's all."

"You're doing what?"

"What, are you deaf or something? I said I'm helping them with their car. Broke down on them. Soon as it's fixed, they're going on to their aunt's house. Right, boy?"

I didn't say anything.

"Are you stupid, or what?" she asked him. When he didn't respond, she glared at him for the longest time without blinking.

"You're gonna have to come up with a better insult than that to offend me," he said.

"When is the last time you had the TV on, you moron? On a news channel."

"I have no electricity, you dumb shit. Or haven't you noticed it's raining?"

"These two kids." She glanced our way. "There's an Amber Alert out for them."

# Chapter 10

"Right," Melvin said with a snigger, like he didn't know whether she was kidding or not. He plopped down on the couch next to one of the buckets full of rainwater, causing the water to splash out.

"What are they doing here?" Rachael demanded.

"I told you. Their car broke down, and I'm helping them. I've got someone—"

"Are you kidding me? So which one was driving? The boy here or the little girl?"

Melvin's sister was clearly upset that we were there. I figured that meant we were in big trouble. I didn't know what an Amber Alert was at the time, and I wasn't sure whether Nurse Ratched was friend or foe. Lucy reached over for my hand, which I grasped with a firm hold.

"The boy drove. He made it all the way from outside of Fulton."

"How old are you?" she asked me.

"Almost thirteen."

She snapped her head back toward Melvin. "You've got to turn them in, Mel. Now."

He squirmed in his seat. "Hey, man, if there's an Amber Alert out for them, that means I could be in a mess of shit."

"You bet your ass you could! What were you thinking?"

"I thought I was helping two kids out of a jam. Something I wish someone had done for me when I was a kid. More than once."

"You've pulled some dumbass shit in your life, but this one gets first prize." She headed for the door. "I'm calling 9-1-1."

"No! Come back here," Melvin shouted on the way to the door. He stood in front of it so she couldn't leave. "Look, I'll come up with something." He stared at me. "You said your aunt lives in Menominee, right, kid?"

"Right."

"And you said you'd recognize her house if you saw it, right?"

"Right."

He turned back to face his sister. "Menominee isn't that big. I'll take them there and drop them off."

"How long have they been here?" she asked.

"Just since yesterday."

"What? They spent the night here?"

"Yeah."

"That's kidnapping, you stupid—"

"Shut the fuck up, Ratched. Let's figure this out. I didn't do anything wrong, and—"

"Don't be an idiot, Mel. You *did* do something wrong. Something *very* wrong. And you're going to have to face the consequences."

"Not if you keep your skinny ass out of it."

"Nice way to talk in front of the kids."

"I'll deliver them to their aunt's house right after dark."

She stood facing him with her feet wide apart, hands on hips. "Number one, you have no way to deliver them anywhere. The road up here is completely washed out."

"How'd you get up here?"

"John's four-wheeler. Number two, the longer you keep them here, the more trouble you'll be in. Three, kidnapping is a felony. It comes with jail time."

"But I didn't know helping a kid was considered kidnapping."

"Tell that to the judge."

"C'mon, Rachael. Help me out here. With my record, I'll be up shit's creek. What harm would there be if I returned them safely to their aunt? Answer me that."

"You've committed a—"

"Answer my question."

"It's irrelevant. You have to do the right thing."

"Put me in jail for trying to help these two kids. You're pathetic, you know that? You sit down there in your high-and-mighty house with your high-and-mighty job, giving me advice. Well, maybe you should think back to when you were young and making one stupid mistake after another, and now you've got three kids to show for it. We all make mistakes, Rachael. And you've made just as many as I have. So get down off your high horse and give me a fucking break. They'll get back to their aunt… tonight…if I have to carry them down on my back to the street and all the way to Menominee."

Lucy let out a wail. "I wanna go home, Benny," she said between sobs.

I cradled her in my arms and stroked her to calm her down.

"Can I say something?" I asked. When neither of them responded, I continued talking. "Melvin did try to help us. He was never mean or anything. And I did some things against the law too. I stole my dad's car. Drove without a license. Took Lucy with me. Maybe they could get me on kidnapping too. I just want for us to get to our aunt's house. She'll take care of us until my parents come home. I know she will. Not calling the police would help me out too. We could end up in foster care…and not together."

Lucy's body stiffened in my arms. "Please don't send us to a faucet house," she cried.

Except for the subtle shaking of her head—back and forth ever so slightly—Rachael stood motionless. After a long few seconds, she sat down on the couch, bowed her head, and closed her eyes. When she looked up, all three of us were staring at her.

No one spoke for the longest moment.

"Let me tell you one thing, Melvin. And listen to me carefully because I'm frickin' serious. If I get into any trouble over this, knowing you're doing the wrong thing and I'm not doing anything about it, I swear I'll kill you."

"You won't, sis. If I get caught, your name will never be mentioned." He turned toward us. "You got that? You can't mention Rachael to anyone… ever."

"I'm good with that," I said. "So is Luce. She'll do whatever I say."

"So we'll hang out here until dark," Melvin said. "Can I use the four-wheeler to get them down to the road?" he asked Rachael.

She nodded and then checked her watch. "Shit! I have to get going. I'm due at the hospital in an hour."

"I'll drive you home in the four-wheeler."

Rachael got up and put on her coat, hesitating a few seconds before opening the door.

"I'll be back in a few minutes," he told us.

* * *

"I'm scared, Benny. What's going to happen to us?"

"When it gets dark out, we're going to take a ride on Rachael's four-wheeler—that should be fun, right? And then Melvin is going to drive us to Aunt Birdie's. And then, you know what?" She shook her head. "This nightmare will be all over. How's that sound?"

"Okay, I guess. Are you hungry?"

"Why? Are you?"

"Yeah."

"When Melvin comes back, we'll ask him if he has anything to eat."

"I still have a half-sandwich from yesterday."

"You want it now?"

"I'm scared I'll throw up."

"You're not feeling well?"

"My stomach has hurted me ever since we left home."

"It will be over soon. I promise."

* * *

Melvin was skittish the whole day—jumping at every sound, looking at us like he was waiting for something to happen, mumbling things under his breath. It made me uncomfortable, and he knew it.

"You kids are nothing but trouble, you know that?" he said sometime in the mid-afternoon.

I didn't respond—too scared to.

"Does she have to cling to you like that?" he asked.

"We're close," I said. "We stick together."

"Wish someone would do that for me. Fuckin' sister I have. I could be knee-deep in horse shit, and she wouldn't throw me a rope." He threw his head in the direction of Lucy. "Would you throw me a rope?" he shouted at her.

Lucy, stunned by his outburst, grabbed on to me even tighter.

"C'mon, you're scaring her," I said. "We'd throw you a rope. Okay?"

Melvin went into his bedroom muttering something about "damn kids" and shut the door. I held on to Lucy the rest of the afternoon.

As soon as the sun went down, we all piled into the four-wheeler along with our big, awkward suitcase and drove along the highest elevation of land leading down to the road. It wasn't easy—the saturated ground caused the vehicle to slip and slide. Once we reached the farmhouse, Melvin parked it and called his buddy Dick to come pick us up.

Dick—older, heavier, and all-around more kempt than Melvin—arrived in his tow truck with our Bronco on the flatbed in back. We piled into the cab. With Lucy on my lap and the suitcase under my feet, it was a tight fit.

"So where to?" he asked in a croaky bullfrog of a voice.

"All they know is that she lives in Menominee, and they'll recognize the house when they see it."

"The road she lives on is a right turn off this road," I told him. "And then it's not that far down."

"Well, there's only one main road into town off Route 20, so we'll try that," Dick said.

"What's with the Bronco," Melvin asked. "Do you know what's wrong with it?"

"Needs brakes. Whoever drove it to that parking lot was smart to leave it there. It's not drivable."

"How much to fix it?"

"With my discount, parts will run under a hundred bucks."

"And labor?"

"A case of beer ought to do it."

Melvin turned at me. "How much money you got?"

"Forty-eight dollars."

He grunted and didn't say anything for several miles.

Dick turned off the highway. "This will bring us into town."

"It's on the right—I know that much," I told them.

"Well, keep your eyes peeled, boy," Melvin said. "We don't need to make a spectacle of ourselves with this big-ass truck."

We had driven by several houses, none that looked familiar, when I spotted the one I thought was hers. "That's it. I'm pretty sure that's her house."

"You're *pretty* sure?"

"Roll down the window, kid. See whose name is on the mailbox."

"Mattis," I said. "That's her!"

"Okay, listen to me," Melvin said to me. "You know not to tell *anyone* about what happened these past two days, right? 'Cause I'll be in a heap of trouble if you do."

"We won't. I promise. And ask anyone, I keep my promises."

"You better, or I'll come looking for you."

"What about our car?" I asked.

"I'll figure something out. It may take a while, but you can't drive it anyway, or you shouldn't. Is there any chance your aunt isn't home? It looks awfully dark in there."

"She's always home. She doesn't drive. Neighbors take her places."

"Okay, buddy. Nice knowin' ya."

"Thanks for all your help, Melvin," I said.

"Want some advice?"

"Sure."

"Don't do anything stupid. Don't end up like me. Don't go driving cars without a license or any shit like that. Just always do the right thing. You'll never go wrong doing that."

"Okay."

I grabbed the suitcase as I climbed out of the cab of the truck. Lucy jumped out and grabbed my free hand, and we walked up Aunt Birdie's driveway without looking back. The sound of Dick's truck pulling away made me feel both relieved and scared at the same time. I couldn't wait to be in our aunt's care, even while I was afraid of how much trouble we'd be in when she found out we'd taken the car and left home on our own.

We walked around to the large patio outside the back door. I rang the doorbell. No response. I knocked as hard as I could.

"Maybe we should go to the front door," I said.

When no one answered the front door, I panicked—so much that I released a little urine into my shorts before I could stop it. I prayed it didn't show.

Lucy peered up at me with wide eyes. "Now what?" she asked.

I stood there feeling lost, afraid, and stupid. I should have asked Melvin and Dick to stay parked on the street until we were safely in the house. When I didn't answer her question, Lucy asked it again, this time with panic in her voice.

"I don't know," I shot back at her. "Let me think."

She sat down on the front stoop and sobbed. "We're never going to get home, Benny."

I sat next to her and put my arm around her shoulder. "Sure we are, Luce. And I'm sorry I yelled at you."

"I'm scared."

"You want to know something?"

"What."

"I'm a little scared too. But the way I figure it, we've got each other, and maybe that's all we've got right now, but it's enough until we get help from Aunt Birdie."

"Where do you think she went?"

"I don't know. Dad said she never went anywhere."

"She did now."

"Maybe she's sleeping and doesn't hear us," I said.

"This early?"

"Sometimes old people take naps. Let's wait by the back door. Maybe the doorbell is broken. I'll try knocking."

When knocking didn't work, we sat on the hard surface of the suitcase on our aunt's patio. The night air was cold and damp, like our house was most of the time. Scant light from a lamppost in the middle of my aunt's small backyard kept us from being completely in the dark.

"I'm cold," Lucy said.

I pulled out a blanket from the suitcase. "Do you want Polly too?"

"Yes, please."

Lucy curled up at my feet and slept while I reflected on things, all kinds of things, until I too fell asleep.

# Chapter 11

"What the—"

A woman's voice, not Aunt Birdie's, awakened me. She stood over us with her hands on her hips, mouth agape.

"Are you Ben, by any chance?" she asked me.

I didn't respond, not fully awake yet.

She smiled. "What are you doing here? Get up. Let me take a look at you."

"Do you know where our aunt is?" I asked as I stood up for her inspection.

She took me by the shoulders and squeezed them a little too hard.

"Are you two okay?"

"Yes. Where's Aunt Birdie?"

"C'mon. Let's go inside. Bring your stuff. And your sister, of course."

I woke up Lucy and told her we could go inside.

"Aunt Birdie's here?" she asked with a huge smile on her face.

"No. Some other lady. Let's go in."

Lucy stood with her feet wide apart, hands on her hips. "Another stranger, Benny?"

"She has a key," I whispered. "She must be a friend of Aunt Birdie's."

"Are you coming, children?" the lady called to us.

"Coming."

We walked into Aunt Birdie's small but tidy kitchen where we found the lady seated at the table, talking on the phone.

"They're here," she said to the person on the other end. "I don't know. I just got here and haven't talked to them yet except to make sure they're okay." She stared at us while she listened to the other party.

"Here," she said as she handed me the phone. "It's your Aunt Birdie."

My tears were unexpected, and I was embarrassed. "Aunt Birdie?" I said through a sob.

"Ben, are you okay? Why are you crying?"

"I'm just glad to hear your voice, that's all."

"Are you okay?"

"I'm okay. Lucy's okay. Where are you?"

"I'm still in the hospital, dear. They may release me tomorrow. We'll see."

"In the hospital! What for?"

"I had a hypoglycemic episode. I'm waiting on test results to see if there was any permanent neurologic damage. All big words, Benjamin. Not to worry." I waited while she spoke to someone who was in her room. "Look, I have to go. More tests. I can't tell you how happy I am to hear your voice, and I'll call you back as soon as I can. In the meantime, Leah will take care of things."

"What things?" I asked, but too late. She'd hung up.

"Is she coming home," Lucy asked.

"As soon as she gets out of the hospital," I told her.

Leah reached toward me for the phone. "Birdie asked me to let the police know you're here."

"Wait!" I said through a gasp. "Don't call them."

She seemed confused. "Why? Do you know there's an Amber Alert out for you? There are people all over this county looking for you."

"Do you have to?"

"Of course, I do. We can't let all of them keep looking for you when you're actually here. What's your concern?"

"We don't want them to take us away," Lucy blurted out.

"Why would they take you away? I can stay here with you until Birdie comes home. I live just around the corner."

A black cat appeared out of nowhere and plodded over to the corner of the kitchen toward a food and water bowl.

"That's Paws."

"Paws?"

"Look at her feet."

"They're huge."

"Hence her name. I've been coming over here a couple times a day to feed her."

"I didn't know Aunt Birdie had a cat," I said.

"She just got her. Keeps her company. Now you've distracted me. I'm going to call the police. Actually, it's the sheriff. Whiteside County Sheriff."

"Wait. You gotta listen to me," I said. "We know enough about these things, believe me. The sheriff will come, and since we are not with a relative, they'll call CPS, and then they'll throw us into foster homes—separate ones. We don't want that. I don't want that…for Lucy."

"Ben, you listen to me. We can't let hundreds of people continue to look for you when you're here. That would be irresponsible. Look, I'll talk to the sheriff and ask him to let you stay here with me until Birdie gets home. I'm sure they're reasonable people."

"But—"

She dialed 9-1-1 and told the person on the other end the whole story. I considered making a mad dash for the door, until I realized I probably wouldn't get very far before being caught, and then I'd be in even more trouble.

After she finished the call, she turned to me. "So where have you—" She stopped mid-sentence. "Never mind. I should leave that for the sheriff."

I didn't like the sound of that. What would I tell them about where we had been without getting Melvin and his sister in trouble? And maybe Dick too. I should have thought that through.

"Lucy, come on. I'll show you where the bathroom is."

"I already know where it is, and I don't have to go."

"No, you don't, and yes, you do. Come on."

I led her into the bathroom and shut the door. "Turn around."

"Not again," she moaned.

"Just do it and listen to me." I talked while I peed. "We can't tell anyone about Melvin, his sister, or Dick. Or Melvin's house. Forget everything Melvin ever said."

"Even his dumb jokes?"

"Even those. What we're going to tell people is that we took the Bronco and drove it up here where it broke down and then some nice lady, we don't know her name, dropped us off here. Do you think you can remember that?"

She shrugged.

"Repeat what I just said. What's our story?"

"That we drove the Bronco. It broke down. And Melvin's sister drove us here."

"No! I told you not to mention them. Pretend we never even met them. Just say some nice lady drove us here."

"Is everything okay in there?" Leah said through the door.

"Out in a minute."

"Got it?" I asked Lucy.

"I think so," she answered. But I was worried.

* * *

Sheriff Joe had a friendly enough face, but I knew that meant nothing when it came to him dragging us off to foster homes. I prayed hard that Leah could convince him to let her take care of us until Aunt Birdie got out of the hospital. After he asked us for the third time if we were okay, Leah chimed in.

"I don't know how much the dispatcher relayed to you about my call, but this is their aunt's house, and of course they'll be living with her until… well, as long as needed. Now, Birdie, their aunt, is in the hospital for a—"

"You may have been misinformed, Miss…what did you say your name was?"

"Leah. Leah Davenport."

"Miss Davenport. That's not exactly how it works. When children are abandoned, Social Services gets involved, and it's a family court judge who determines where they're placed. Now, their aunt can file a petition to be their caregiver, and if she meets their standards, I'm sure the court will consider her, but until that—"

"What standards?" Leah asked.

"Financial stability, suitable home environment, valid driver's license, insurance. They have to pass a criminal background check. Stuff like that."

"I was hoping they could stay with me, here, until Birdie takes over."

"No can do. Social Services will be here shortly, and—"

"No!" Lucy shouted as she ran to my side. "I'm not going!"

# Chapter 12

When two women, both social workers, showed up at Aunt Birdie's house within twenty minutes of Sheriff Joe's arrival, I knew we were doomed—the thing I had been most afraid would happen was actually playing out, and there was not a thing I could do about it. I wasn't so worried about my own placement but couldn't bear the thought of Lucy being sent off to live with some strange family. I let her cling to me, hoping she didn't feel me shaking.

"I'm Mrs. Underbrink," the taller of the two women said, "and this is Mrs. Brownback. And how are you children doing today?"

I so wanted to tell her that that was a really stupid question.

"Fine," I said.

Mrs. Brownback walked over to us and held out her hand to Lucy. "Would you like to come with me in the other room where we can get to know each other?"

Lucy stiffened and clung to me even tighter.

"We'd like to stay together, if it's all the same to you," I said.

"Well, we think it's better if we talk to you separately. So there are no distractions and so each of you fully understands what's going to happen."

I didn't like her voice—dripping with kindness, whispery, like in a commercial where the person doing the voiceover is talking about something personal, like toilet paper.

"We'll understand just fine," I told her.

"Now, Benjamin, we have certain—"

"Look, lady. My sister is scared to death. I'm her big brother, and she needs me right now. So back off. And another thing, we will *not* be separated. You separate us, and I'll just run away and come find her. And just so you know, I'm pretty good at finding things."

Mrs. Underbrink motioned for the other lady to come with her to another room. After a few minutes, they returned.

"Okay, we'll talk to both of you at the same time," she said. "Let me start by saying that some very special people have been chosen to look after you until your mother is…able to take care of you. Or a close relative. Your foster parents will provide you with—"

"You know where our mother is?" I asked.

The two women gazed at each other, and then Mrs. Underbrink nodded.

"Benjamin, I'm afraid your mother has been incarcerated."

"What does that mean?" I asked.

"She's in jail."

As soon as she said it, Leah left the room.

Lucy bawled. "No, she's not!" she shouted into my shirt. "Stop lying."

I sat in silence while I processed this new piece of information. "Why? What did she do?" I asked, trying to ignore the rock-like feeling in my stomach and struggling not to cry.

"She's been charged with theft."

That didn't sound like our mother. "What did she steal?"

"I don't know the details."

"She has a bail hearing tomorrow," Sheriff Joe added.

"And our dad? Is he with her?"

"No, son. He's not."

"Where is he?"

The three adults in the room eyed each other.

Leah came back into the room. "Excuse me, ladies, may I talk with one of you privately please? And Sheriff Joe, will you join us?"

Mrs. Brownback stayed behind.

"Where's my dad?" I asked her in a tone I knew she wouldn't appreciate.

"I don't know, son."

"Don't call me son."

"I'm sorry. I shouldn't have said that, Ben."

We sat in silence while the three other adults whispered in the kitchen. They returned with solemn faces.

"Mrs. Underbrink, would you like to finish your talk?" the sheriff asked.

"What I had started to tell you was—"

"Where's my dad?"

"We can't talk about him right now, Benjamin. That's for a later time. Now, what I was about to say was—"

"Why won't you tell me?"

"It's rude to keep interrupting. May I finish my talk now?" She didn't wait for a response. "As I was saying—"

"This stinks."

Mrs. Underbrink pursed her lips, her face growing progressively redder as she continued.

"We have found a special place for you to stay. With nice families. We're right at the beginning of a school year, so changing schools shouldn't be a problem."

"We don't go to school."

"I beg your pardon."

"We're homeschooled."

"Well, then, you're in for a big treat because we don't homeschool in foster homes. And then—"

"You're going to separate us, aren't you?"

"Benjamin, we try to keep siblings together, but it's not always possible, especially on such short notice. There are no foster homes in this area that can take on two children."

"Shows how much they like children, doesn't it?"

"It's not that. Sometimes there aren't enough bedrooms, or they can't afford to take two children. There could be all sorts of reasons."

"They get paid for taking care of us—that much I know."

"You're right. They do get paid, but they also spend a considerable amount of their own money. Look, these are people who came to us and said they want to help a child, add to their own family. No one asked them to—they volunteered."

I hated her.

"In your new home, Ben, there's another boy about your age. Won't that be fun?"

I ignored the question.

"And there are seven-year-old twin girls in Lucy's new home and a dog. Do you like dogs, Lucy?"

"I hate dogs!"

She didn't really.

"It's getting late and time to go."

"Who do I talk to about Mom and Dad when I'm there? How will I know what's going on? Will I have Lucy's phone number? Can we see each other?"

"You will have a social worker assigned to you. You can ask her anything you like. If she doesn't know the answer, she'll find out and get back to you."

"And Lucy?"

"She'll have one too. I'll do what I can to see that you both get the same social worker. That should help with communication between you and your sister."

Mrs. Brownback walked over to us and tried to pry Lucy from me.

"I won't go!" she screamed. "Benny, do something!"

"Does she have any other clothes?" Mrs. Brownback shouted to be heard over Lucy's screams. "Any other belongings?"

I removed everything of Lucy's from the suitcase, being careful not to reveal any of the items I'd found under my parents' closet. I left Lucy's things in a pile on the floor, forcing Mrs. Brownback to bend over and pick them up.

As long as I live, I'll never forget Lucy being carried out the front door kicking and screaming, "You promised me, Benny! You promised." I could imagine what was going through her terrified mind—her disappointment in me, her feeling of betrayal.

It was one thing to fail at something like school or in some sport where you might get a second chance to do better, but there were no do-overs in protecting your little sister.

# Chapter 13

"Would you mind if I spent a few minutes alone with Benjamin, Mrs. Underbrink?" Sheriff Joe asked.

"I'll be in the car," she responded.

"So…I know this is upsetting, but you'll see that in time, it will get better. Change is always hard at first."

"It's mean what you guys are doing. Just plain mean."

He stared at me for a long moment, maybe looking for more of what he thought were the right words to say to me. He probably didn't know that in my mind nothing he said to me would have been right.

He took out a pen and small notebook from his breast pocket. "I have to write up a report on this incident, so I need a couple of facts from you. Is that okay?"

"Do I need a lawyer?"

He smiled. "You're not being charged with anything. May I continue?"

"Do I have a choice?"

Another long stare. "I'm here to help you, you know. I'm on your side."

He would have had a hard time convincing me of that.

"Let's go back in time. How did you get here, to your aunt's house?"

"This lady drove us here."

"Her name?"

"Don't know."

"Just some stranger?"

"Yep."

"What did she look like?"

"I don't know. Just a regular lady."

"How old would you say?"

"Older. Like a grandma."

"What kind of car did she have?"

"Uh, kind of small."

"Color?"

"Red."

"She picked you up at your house?"

"No."

"Where then?"

"Casey's."

"Casey's General Store?"

"Yes."

"The one in Galena?"

"I think so. I'm not sure."

"How did you get there?"

"I drove."

Sheriff Joe peered over the rim of his glasses. "You drove."

"Yes."

"You drove what?"

"My dad's Bronco."

"Where did you learn to drive?"

"My dad."

"You drove from your house to Galena?"

"To Casey's…if that's in Galena."

"What day was this?"

"Today." The more I lied, the tighter the knot in my stomach became.

"Where were you yesterday?"

"Home."

"Ben, we've been to your home every day since Friday when your aunt notified us. You weren't there."

"We were hiding."

"Hiding. Where?"

"In the storm cellar."

"We checked there."

"It was locked."

"We broke the lock."

"Isn't that against the law?" I didn't know where the courage was coming from to talk to him like that.

"When we think someone's life is in danger, we'll break down doors to get to them. Now, where were you hiding?"

"In the secret room in the closet." I hadn't wanted to reveal this to him, to anyone, but I felt cornered.

"Tell me about it."

"In my parents' bedroom, in the closet, on the floor, there's a trap door and steps down to a secret room."

"And you hid there, knowing law enforcement was upstairs looking for you?"

"We didn't know who it was. We were scared."

Sheriff Joe shook his head. "Okay, so you hid in this secret room each time we came?"

"Yes."

"And then you drove your dad's Bronco to Galena where this nice lady picked you up. How did she know to pick you up there? And why did she pick you up? Why not drive the rest of the way yourself?"

"It broke down."

"The Bronco?"

"Mm-hm."

"At Casey's?"

I nodded.

"And the lady in the red car?"

"She just happened to be driving by, I guess, and asked if we needed help."

"And you said what?"

"That we needed a ride here."

"Didn't she think it was a little odd that a twelve-year-old was driving a car?"

I shrugged. "Maybe she didn't know it was our car."

"When she drove you here and found your aunt wasn't here, what did she say?"

"She didn't know our aunt wasn't here. She just dropped us off."

"So this nice lady dropped off two young, unsupervised kids, to a house she had no way of knowing was occupied by a loving aunt or a gang of thugs. She just left you there."

"Yep."

The sheriff let out an audible sigh. "And then what?"

"We hung out on her patio waiting for her."

"But she never came."

"No. Leah came over to feed the cat and found us there."

"And what happened to your car?"

"Still there, as far as I know."

"Do you have the keys?"

"Uh…I…I left them in the car." I lied.

"Why'd you do that?"

"Wasn't thinking, I guess."

"I guess not. Did you at least lock it?"

"I think so."

He finished writing and stood up.

"I've heard enough for now. I may be back in touch, though. Come on, I'll walk you to the car."

* * *

I remained silent in the back seat of Mrs. Underbrink's car during the drive to my foster home—staring out the window in a zombie-like state into the dark night. Another social worker sat beside me. Apparently, they thought it would take two of them to transport me there. They were probably right.

My mind kept going back to the image of Lucy being dragged off to some unfamiliar place—the sounds of her screams piercing to my sensibilities. I tried not to think about how scared she had to be, how lonely and distraught.

In less than twenty minutes, we reached our destination. It appeared nice enough from the outside—a small, one-story clapboard house with a carport instead of a garage. White picket fence. I approached the front door, flanked on each side by a social worker. When it opened, a woman around my mom's age stood there smiling.

"Come right on in, Benjamin. I'm Mrs. Putnam. Welcome to our home." More sugar and spice.

The man I assumed was Mr. Putnam remained seated in a recliner reading the paper.

"David, come meet Benjamin."

Mr. Putnam lowered the paper, mumbled something I didn't understand, and continued with his reading.

After the three women had a whispery tête-à-tête near the front door, the two social workers left.

"Our son, Patrick, is still in bed. It's quite early, you know. Not many people are up at this hour. You'll meet him a little later. Won't that be nice, having a brother around? I understand you're twelve. Patrick's nine. I think the two of you will get along just fine. Are you hungry, dear? Can I get you something to eat? To drink?"

Already I was tired of hearing her talk.

"I'd like to go to bed, if that's alright with you."

"Of course, it is. I'll show you to your room."

She led the way through the house. It didn't look very lived in—not a lot of stuff lying around.

"It's a nice room. I think you'll like it. It was our other son's room. He died, you know. Lung infection, then pneumonia. So young. Too young to die like that. Sometimes God works in mysterious ways. Do you go to church, Benjamin? Sunday school? If not, that's okay. We have a very nice church in town and… But let's not get into that right now."

I didn't know how she managed to get that much said in such a short hallway, but she did.

The room was small, which I didn't mind. After all, I had never had a room of my own before—of any size. What I did mind was that it appeared that all of her dead son's things still occupied it—soccer trophies, Cubs poster on the wall, a Nintendo console, a pair of shoes on the floor.

"I hope you like your room. It's just the way Phillip left it."

*My* room. It didn't feel much like *my* room.

"You can put your suitcase in this corner, and if you want to hang up your clothes, I made room in the closet, next to Phillip's clothes. Mr. Putnam and I talked about it, and we decided if you want to play with Phillip's Nintendo, you can. We don't think he'd mind. Is there anything you need, dear? Oh, wait, let me show you the bathroom."

I followed her to a door next to the closet. "It's a Jack-and-Jill, so Patrick can come in from the other side. You two can work out a schedule in the morning, so you're not running into each other. He and Phillip did that, and it worked out just fine. Just—"

I left the bathroom before she finished.

"I know how stressful this must be for you. Now, if you ever want to talk about it, I'm here for you. And so is Mr. Putnam. We can talk any time. And your social worker—I haven't been told who that is yet—will also be available for you. Sometimes it helps to talk to someone outside the home. Are you okay?"

Stupid question.

I nodded.

"Good night, then."

"Good night."

# Chapter 14

The first thing I did in Phillip's bedroom was hide the stuff I'd found under my parents' closet. After inspecting the room, I put the figurines and other items in the cedar chest under the window, buried beneath several blankets. Next, I rummaged around in Phillip's desk for paper and pencil to make a list of questions for the social worker, like when I would be able to talk to Lucy, when Aunt Birdie was coming home, how long Mom would be in jail, and where my dad was.

As I lay on Phillip's bed, my mind drifted to Melvin and what he was doing with the Bronco, and that train of thought led me to worry about Sheriff Joe and what he would think when he went to Casey's and saw the Bronco wasn't there.

Sheriff Joe. I was pretty sure he didn't believe much, maybe not any, of the story I'd given him about how we'd gotten to Aunt Birdie's. It occurred to me that if he ever asked Lucy the same questions, we'd be in big trouble.

Lucy. No six-year-old should have to go through the whole foster care thing alone, and I felt it was all my fault. I had always watched over her—that was my job. If I had been better at it, the two of us wouldn't have been in the mess we were in. At least, that's what my twelve-year-old mind thought at the time. It wasn't until much later that I understood the limitations I was under.

I looked for someone else to blame. Mom—she had gotten herself locked up. Unless she didn't actually do what they said she'd done, then I could blame the police. Or Dad. Mom had an excuse for not coming to get us, but what about him? Where was he when we needed him?

I worried about having to go to school. Mom had never pushed us to do much at home. What if all the other kids were smarter than me? What if they put me in a lower grade with younger kids? I'd feel like a fool. According to her age, Lucy would be in first grade. I'd be in seventh.

I worried about how long we'd have to stay in these homes before Aunt Birdie could take us in or my dad showed up.

I worried about all of this until I fell asleep.

* * *

I awoke to a pajama-clad boy staring at me.

"Do you need something?" I asked him.

He shook his head.

"Do you mind, then? I'd like to get dressed."

The boy, who I assumed was Patrick, disappeared through our shared bathroom. The clock on the dresser said six a.m.

I gathered some clothes and, pleased to see a lock on the inside of both bathroom doors, I showered and dressed. When I finished, I found Mrs. Putnam scurrying around her rooster-themed kitchen.

"Good morning, Benjamin," she said. "Should I call you that? Or do you go by a nickname? We don't use nicknames in our family, but if you want to use one, that's okay. Like Ben. Or any other nickname. Did you sleep okay? How did you find the bed? Phillip liked that bed. I'm making scrambled eggs for breakfast. Do you like scrambled eggs?"

She may have said more—I tuned a lot of it out, smiling and nodding when appropriate. In the midst of her jabbering, Patrick joined us.

"I'd like to meet with my social worker today, if that's okay," I told her.

"Have you two met yet?" she asked. "Patrick, this is Benjamin. Benjamin, this is Patrick. The school bus picks Patrick up on the corner at seven-thirty. He has to go all the way to East Dubuque. So will you, as soon as we get you enrolled."

I tried to make eye contact with Patrick, but he seemed more interested in the empty place setting before him.

"I'd like to meet with my social worker today," I repeated.

She was standing in front of the stove with her back to me and seemed not to hear me. "It's a good school. Our Phillip went there too. Just loved it. He was in—"

"Mrs. Putnam!" I shouted, regretting it soon after.

She whipped herself around to face me. "What's the matter?"

"I'm sorry. I didn't mean to yell, but I asked you twice if I could meet with my social worker today."

She walked toward me as she dried her hands on a dish towel. "We don't yell in this house, Benjamin. Is that clear?"

"I said I was sorry. Now can you answer my question?"

She turned to Patrick. "Please share the house rules with Benjamin later today."

Patrick didn't respond, at least not verbally.

"Now, to get back to your question, I'll have to check the *Foster Care Handbook* to see how I should handle communication with your social worker."

She gave me no timeframe, and I didn't ask, thinking I'd better familiarize myself with the house rules first.

She joined us at the table. "You might be wondering where Mr. Putnam is," she said. "Mr. Putnam is an accountant, and he likes to get an early start to his day at the office, so you probably won't see him in the morning."

I was thinking that if I were him I would get out of the house early too.

"Let us pray," she said as she bowed her head.

I wasn't expecting that. I didn't come from a praying family.

After she said a prayer that included thanking God for bringing me to their family, she picked up where she'd left off with her incessant talking.

"Are your eggs okay? I don't scramble them too hard or they end up rubbery. Phillip liked them that way. You do too, right, Patrick?"

She didn't look at me when she talked, which drove me crazy—I couldn't let her know by facial expression that I wanted to speak. I took a chance and slid in a question when she took a breath. "May I talk to the social worker today?"

"And then we'll look through your suitcase and see that you have proper clothes for school and for church." She gave me a once-over. "We want you to appear neat and clean at school—first impressions are so important."

"May I *please* talk to the social worker today?"

"I wonder if Phillip's clothes would fit you. You're large for twelve, and he was, well, more normal."

After she used the phrase "more normal" to compare me to her dead son, I completely tuned her out.

* * *

Based on what Mom had done for us when it came to homeschooling, I figured maybe my aunt could do the same thing. But trying to convince Mrs. Putnam to hold off registering me for school until we knew when Aunt Birdie was coming home proved to be a waste of time. She listened to no one. I didn't know how Mr. Putnam or Patrick put up with her constant talking. Less than twenty-four hours after arriving there, I was ready to bolt.

Finally, after dinner on my first full day with the Putnams, she told me that my social worker would be Mrs. Brownback and that we had been scheduled to meet on Thursday evening. I didn't want to wait two more days to talk with her.

"I have questions, Mrs. Putnam. Important questions. I feel like I'm in the dark here."

"Well, Benjamin, I'm sorry you feel that way. We've provided a nice place for you to live, a comfortable bed, plenty of food. I even let you wear Phillip's clothes."

I wanted to throw something at her. What did that have to do with my questions? And I hated having to try on Phillip's clothes. They didn't fit me, but still she expected me to wear them. I wanted to shout at her to stop comparing me to him. I wasn't Phillip.

"And when we were interviewed by the foster care people, they said—"

"I'm sorry to interrupt," I said, knowing it was the wrong thing to do. "I'm sure interrupting is against the rules, but my questions have nothing to do with your home, or you, or anything here. They have to do with my family."

"We went through a rigorous vetting process that—"

"Listen to the boy, for crissake, Emma," Mr. Putnam said from another room. Those were the first audible words I'd heard him speak.

"Humph!" she uttered through pursed lips.

"What are your questions, Benjamin?" she asked in a voice much softer than her usual penetrating tone.

I had no desire to discuss my business with her, but under the circumstances, I figured I'd better go along with it. From my shirt pocket, I pulled the list I'd made.

"When is Aunt Birdie getting out of the hospital, and can I talk to her on the phone or visit her in the meantime?" I glanced up at Mrs. Putnam but got no response, so I continued. "Can I talk to my sister, Lucy, on the phone or visit with her? How long does my mother have to stay in jail? Where is my father?"

I refolded the list, put it back in my pocket, and waited for someone to say something.

The phone rang. When Mrs. Putnam came back from the kitchen after taking the call, she had a smug look on her face.

"Sheriff DeLawter wants to stop by in an hour." Her glare made me shiver. "To talk to you."

"Good. Maybe *he* can answer my questions," I said before rising from my chair. "I'll be in Phillip's room until the sheriff gets here."

# Chapter 15

After Sheriff Joe entered Phillip's bedroom and sat down on the cedar chest, I willed myself to not think about all the figurines in weird sexual poses that were right under his butt.

"I know you have some questions for me, Ben, but I wonder if I could ask you a few first."

"Sure," I said. I had a strong feeling about what he wanted to ask me.

"We checked the parking lot of Casey's General Store. The white Bronco you said you drove there is not there."

"It isn't?"

"No, it isn't. How do you explain that?"

I shrugged. "That's where we left it."

"One of the clerks who works there told me he saw two kids, one about your age and one about your sister's age, standing by a white SUV in the parking lot on Sunday, in the middle of the night. You said you drove there on Monday. Something is not adding up."

"Maybe it wasn't us he saw."

"Pretty unlikely." His stare frightened me.

"Maybe he was wrong about the day."

"I thought that too, so I asked him about it, and he checked his time card. He didn't work on Monday."

I hoped nothing on the outside of my body reflected what was shaking on the inside.

"You wouldn't have any reason to lie to me, would you?"

"No."

"Because I'm here to tell you that it's always best to tell the truth up-front. If it comes out later, well, things can go badly. Do you understand that?"

"Yes."

"Whose car did you say it was?"

"The Bronco?"

"Yes, that's the one we're discussing."

"My dad's."

"Well, I checked that too. There's no Bronco registered to your father."

"It was sitting next to our shed for as long as I can remember."

"Were there plates on it?"

I shrugged.

"Mm-hm. One more question. This lady who you said picked you up at Casey's, describe her car to me again."

"It was red and kind of small."

"Checked that out too. There are no small red cars registered in Whiteside, Lee, Winnebago, Carroll, or Ogle counties. Not a one."

"Maybe she was from somewhere else. Wisconsin even."

"Right."

I didn't know where to focus my eyes when he wasn't talking, so I looked down.

"That's all I have for now. What questions do you have for me?"

I was hoping he'd forgotten about my questions—I wasn't sure my stomach could take any more of him. I retrieved the list from my pocket and trusted I could keep enough composure to get through it.

"When is my mom getting out of jail?"

"She had her bail hearing this morning, but she wasn't granted bail."

"What does that mean?"

He explained it to me, but all I heard was that she had to stay in jail until her court case, and that could take months.

"When is Aunt Birdie coming home?"

"I talked to your Aunt Birdie, and she thinks by Friday, but she can't be sure."

"Can I talk to her?"

"I don't see why not. Mrs. Putnam should be able to arrange that for you. I'll let her know what hospital your aunt is in."

"How about my sister? Can I see her? Talk to her?"

"Well, that's up to your social worker. You'll have to ask her."

"How do I get in touch with her?"

"Your foster mom knows how to reach her."

Not the answer I wanted to hear.

"Anything else?"

"Do you know where my dad is?"

"Your aunt wants to talk to you about your dad."

"So you're not going to tell me?"

"Like I said, your aunt wants to do that."

He rose from the cedar chest and put on his official sheriff's hat.

"I'll be back in touch," he said on his way out.

A few minutes after he left, someone, presumably Patrick, slid several sheets of paper under my bedroom door. THE HOUSE RULES. I read the first one. NO PHYSICAL OR VERBAL ABUSE TOWARD ANYONE (THAT INCLUDES RAISING ONE'S VOICE). I'd already violated that one. When I saw fifty more rules listed, I put the paper down for a later time, when I was more up for it.

* * *

"Aunt Birdie?"

"Yes, dear. It's me. It's good to hear your voice," she said over the phone. Mrs. Putnam had made the call and handed me the phone, like I wasn't capable of making the call myself. Now, she sat across the kitchen table, listening to my side of the conversation.

"Same here. How are you feeling?"

"Better. Much better."

"Do you know when you're coming home?"

"Friday at the earliest, they tell me."

"And then we can come stay with you until…"

Her sigh was audible, even over the phone. "That's what I want to happen, Ben. But it's not that easy. It's my understanding that CPS has to make that decision, and first they have to inspect my home, interview me, look at my finances—a whole lot of things they take into consideration. So let's not jump the gun. You're in a safe place now. We better take this one step at a time. Okay?"

I didn't see where I had much choice.

"Okay. Aunt Birdie?"

"Yes."

"I know about Mom."

"Yes, I know. Leah told me."

"Do you know what she stole?"

"No, dear, I don't."

"Where is Dad?"

When she didn't respond, I repeated the question.

"Benjamin, I'm afraid I have some very bad news for you. I didn't want to tell you this over the phone, but you have the right to know."

I braced myself for the worst.

"Your father, my brother, was involved in a terrible car accident, and he…he…I'm so sorry, Ben. He…"

She didn't have to finish the sentence. I knew he was dead.

# Chapter 16

I handed the phone back to Mrs. Putnam without saying goodbye and ran to my room, a massive sob welling up in my throat and numbness blocking any specific thoughts about my father.

Hours later, she came in to ask me if I needed anything. I had to struggle to keep from yelling at her. I had just been told my father was dead. What did she think I needed? I managed to contain myself, but right then, I hated that woman.

Dinner time came and went. Mrs. Putnam slipped a tray of food into my room, but I had no interest in it. I remember thinking how unfair life had been to me the past week—given all I'd been through—and it didn't seem to be getting any better.

Over the years, I've learned there's really no point in getting too angry about unfairness. It was always better in the end to accept it and adjust accordingly. But back then, I didn't know how to deal with my father being dead. With our mother in jail, it seemed like Lucy and I faced a pretty bleak and hopeless future. And we'd have to navigate through our current situations separately for a while—at least until Aunt Birdie was approved to take care of us.

I felt so alone—it was one thing to be alone and not know the whereabouts of your parents or when they were coming home, but an entirely different thing to know where they were and that they were not coming home. At least with unknowns, there was hope.

Being anywhere but at the Putnams' seemed preferable to me. Even Melvin's was more appealing. At least I had been able to talk to the guy.

Mrs. Talkaholic never let anyone get a word in, and even when they did, she didn't hear what they had to say.

I was so counting on Aunt Birdie.

* * *

I awoke physically tired and mentally drained. It was Wednesday, the day Mrs. Putnam was to take me to school for testing to determine what grade I'd be in—the last thing I wanted to do that day. Well, maybe not the last thing—I still had to endure the ride with her there …and back.

When we arrived at the school, an older woman with no smile and a tight bun on the top of her head that resembled a napping cat from a distance led me to an empty classroom and told me I had three hours to complete the test. She sat at the teacher's desk and stared at me until I glanced down at the stack of papers before me.

In Part I, I had to write a 100- to 150-word composition on one of the following subjects:

- My mother
- My father
- My best friend
- An interesting trip
- My pet

Let's see—my mother was in jail. My father was dead. I had no friends except my sister, who had been separated from me by brute force. My most interesting trip involved me stealing a car and driving forty miles without a driver's license. And I didn't have a pet. I'd never had a pet.

I peeked at Part II, Reading Comprehension. It looked easier than Part I, so I started there. All I had to do was read a short story and answer some multiple-choice questions afterward. Simple stuff. Then I found four more short stories to read, with each set of multiple-choice questions growing progressively more difficult. I blew off the last one—a story about the American Revolutionary War. How did France aid the Patriot cause? Even with multiple-choice answers and having read it twice, I didn't have a clue.

The last part of this section was simply unfair—a poem titled "Daffodils." With a beginning like "I wandered lonely as a cloud that floats on high o'er vales and hills," I had no hope, so I ticked off random answers.

By the time I finished the rest of the test—grammar, punctuation, and math—I was pretty sure that I wasn't going to be placed in the seventh grade. After I turned it in and we were walking to Mrs. Putnam's car, I remembered that I hadn't gone back to complete Part I—the composition.

* * *

Taking the placement test took my mind off my father's death, but that changed the minute I finished it. After pumping me in the car about how I did on the test, Mrs. Putnam took on the role of grief counselor.

"Grief is a healthy process, Benjamin. It's okay to grieve for as long as you want. Don't be embarrassed by it just because you're a boy."

Even at twelve, I knew that much.

"Think about the good times you had with him."

My father had sat around all day drinking beer. A good time was when he passed out early and we didn't have to tiptoe around him.

"How he helped you become the young man you are today."

I was a car thief, drove without a license, and evaded the authorities.

"The love he had for your mother."

I never saw them hug or kiss, just argue.

"I can help you make a memory box, if you like."

I wanted to tell her to give it up, that she wasn't helping. But I didn't.

* * *

The social worker, Mrs. Brownback, paid us a visit on Thursday evening, as promised. The pained look on her face told me she was about to give me bad news.

"I have the results of your placement test, Benjamin. According to your test scores, they think you should be placed in the fifth grade—conditionally, depending on how you do there."

"What!" I had mentally prepared myself to be put back one grade, not two.

"I know that's not what you wanted to hear, but based on your scores, that's—"

"I am *not* going into the fifth grade with a bunch of ten-year-olds."

"Sometimes we have no choice in matters. We have to—"

"I won't go. That's all there is to it."

"You *will* go. It's the law."

"Why can't I be homeschooled like before?"

"I don't believe in homeschooling," Mrs. Putnam chimed in.

"Why not? It worked for us just fine."

"Apparently, it didn't," Mrs. Brownback said. "You tested in the tenth percentile among your peers."

"What does that mean?"

"It means out of a hundred children your age, you scored lower than ninety of them."

"Aunt Birdie used to be a schoolteacher. She can do it. And she'll do it right."

"But your aunt isn't available to do it."

"But she will be."

"There are a lot of 'ifs' involved here, Benjamin. If she comes home from the hospital, if she's qualified to foster you, if she can homeschool you. We have to think of *now*. We're not going to let you avoid school until other arrangements can be made. You've already missed a few weeks of the school year."

"Well, this stinks."

"It may not be ideal," Mrs. Putnam said. "But it's the best arrangement we have available to us."

"When do I have to go?"

"Monday."

"How am I going to get there?"

"On the same bus as Patrick."

"Great—I'll be one grade ahead of a nine-year-old."

"Actually, Patrick is in the fifth grade too. He skipped a grade."

She couldn't have told me anything more disheartening.

Mrs. Putnam left the room to answer the phone.

"And now I want to talk to you about Lucy," Mrs. Brownback said. "She's—"

"I want to see her."

"What I was going to say is that her social worker thinks it's best if you don't see her...not yet."

"Why?"

"She needs time to adjust."

"That's not fair!" I said, slamming my fist on the table.

"Remember the rules, Benjamin," Mrs. Putnam said from the other room.

"Fuck the rules!" I yelled and stomped to my room, slamming the door as hard as I could behind me, breaking yet more of the stupid "house rules."

The whole thing seemed so wrong. How could whoever was in charge of where kids lived be so cruel? Here I was, bigger than most twelve-year-olds to begin with, forced to go to school with a bunch of ten-year-olds…and a nine-year-old. And Lucy and I belonged together. All we had was each other. And how did I know if she was really being well taken care of, if she was okay? Why didn't they want me to see her—so I wouldn't see how bad off she was? If Dad had been there, he'd have told them all to go to hell… or something.

But then I realized, if Dad had been there, I wouldn't have been in this mess.

Remembering a TV special about some kid suing his parents, I wondered who I could sue.

* * *

After receiving a long scolding from Mrs. Putnam about my behavior with the social worker, half of which I didn't hear because I tuned her out, I retreated to my room to think things through. Dad would never be coming home, it was uncertain when Mom was coming home, and Aunt Birdie wasn't as much of a sure thing as I'd once thought. After I got over the initial shock of being placed in the fifth grade, I came around to thinking maybe I'd better go along with everything, put on a good show, to make my life bearable until things could get back on track. I only hoped that living with the Putnams wasn't going to end up being the "track" I was destined for.

Friday ended without any word from Aunt Birdie. On Saturday morning, Mrs. Putnam knocked on my door and opened it before I had a chance to invite her in, a habit of hers I had come to resent.

"Can I talk to you, Benjamin?"

"Sure."

"Leah Davenport called to let me know they're keeping your aunt in the hospital a few more days. I thought you might want to know that."

She thought I might want to know that? The most important issue in my life at the time, and she thought I might want to know?

"Is she alright?" I asked.

"I think they're concerned about her having seizures and want to observe her for a while longer."

"What are seizures?"

"That's when your brain goes haywire or something and you get all spacey and then go blind. Actually, I'm not sure. Maybe not all people are like that. She's in good hands, though. Our Phillip was in that same hospital."

Where he died.

I had been worried about my aunt *before* that conversation. Now, I was in panic mode.

# Chapter 17

With only two days before I had to show my twelve-year-old face in a fifth-grade classroom, my stomach had become a jumbled mess, and having Patrick in the same class made the situation ten times worse. I pictured myself towering over the other kids, struggling with homework, Mrs. Putnam comparing Patrick's grades to mine and telling Patrick to help me. It couldn't have been any more degrading and embarrassing.

I was angry at Mom for homeschooling me and at Dad for dying. No one had ever mentioned drunk driving in regard to his car accident, but I knew that was a likely scenario.

It had been only ten days since I'd last seen my parents, even though it seemed a lot longer, yet I couldn't picture either of them in my mind, and that was unsettling. I knew I'd never see my dad again, but I worried that I might never see my mom again either. She'd figure we were in a good home and forget about us. Or maybe she'd die in jail. I had seen that happen on TV more than once.

Just when I figured I was done with Sheriff Joe, he appeared at the Putnams' door one Saturday morning. Mrs. Putnam called me into the living room.

"I just went by your Aunt Birdie's house, and guess what I found," the sheriff said.

"She's home!?"

"No. Afraid not. But your Ford Bronco is."

A wave of fear rippled through my body. "It is?"

"Mm-hm. I was hoping you'd be able to tell me how it got there."

"I've been here," I said.

"I know that. Would you like to tell me who drove it there?"

I shrugged. "I don't know."

"I think you do."

"Tell him the truth, Benjamin," Mrs. Putnam interjected. "We don't lie in this house."

"How would I know who drove it there if I've been here the whole time?"

"The question is, Who knew to drive it to your aunt's house? That must be a very small group of people, wouldn't you agree? It had to be someone who knows you."

I shrugged.

"Let's start with a list of everyone who knew that it was your father's car."

"Lucy and me."

"Keep going."

"Our mom."

"Who else?"

"Aunt Birdie?"

"We know it wasn't her."

"I don't know anyone else."

"Come on, Ben, there had to be other people who knew about that Bronco. It's a collector's car, for one thing."

"I think that's why my dad bought it."

"Bought it?"

"Yeah."

"No plates or registration. VIN number etched off."

"Huh?"

"VIN number—vehicle identification number. All vehicles have one. They're usually etched off if the car is stolen so no one can trace the car to its rightful owner."

"I don't know anything about that," I told him.

He stared at me for several seconds—never once blinking—before he spoke. "I have to wait seventy-two hours before I can consider it an abandoned car."

"What happens to it then?" I asked.

"It'll be towed to a secure lot where we have to keep it for a period of time before it's destroyed."

I nodded.

"Don't get any ideas, kid. I took the keys out of it."

"I wouldn't do anything like that, Sheriff Joe. I learned my lesson," I said, even though that had been my first thought—why destroy a perfectly good car?

The sheriff rose, tipped his hat, and left. I figured that wasn't going to be the last time I had to deal with Sheriff Joe.

* * *

I dreaded Sunday—going-to-church day. I had never stepped inside of a church, and to the best of my knowledge neither had my parents. The four of us piled into the Putnams' Buick station wagon and headed for Crossroads Community Church.

"I know you'll like our church, Benjamin. Our Phillip did. And so do you, don't you, Patrick? The sermon last week was all about patience. Imagine, a whole sermon about patience. Do you know what it means to be patient, Benjamin? It means you put up with bad times without complaining. Suffer through them. But it's even more than that—you can turn that suffering to something positive. Not many people do that, you know. Like Jacob, for example…"

I tuned her out as I silently prayed for patience.

After church, Mr. Putnam drove to Casey's General Store in Galena where the four of us shared a medium-sized breakfast pizza that I could easily have eaten all by myself.

"We came here for two reasons," said Mrs. Putnam after saying her usual mealtime prayer. "First of all, it's always a treat when Mr. Putnam brings us here for breakfast after church. But we also thought it might jar your memory a little about your car. We think the sheriff would like to know more about it."

"I told him everything I know."

"I see. Well, take your time eating. Maybe something will come to mind."

By then, I had finished my allotted one slice of pizza, so all I could do was sit there looking stupid. RULE 36: DON'T SPEAK UNLESS SPOKEN TO DURING MEALS.

* * *

The first day of school arrived too soon. With my newfound religious guidance, I had prayed for some kind of miracle to happen so I wouldn't have to go, but the praying didn't work.

Patrick and I stood on the corner with a few other kids, all younger and much smaller than me, waiting for the bus.

"What grade are you in?" a wide-eyed little girl in a red dress and white sneakers asked me.

I ignored her.

She tugged on my sleeve. "What grade are you in?"

"Fifth." *Now go away.*

"Really?"

*Yes, really. Where's the damn bus?*

"I'm in first," she said.

"That's nice."

"What's your name?"

"Albert Schweitzer." This name, which had appeared in one of the sucky test questions that had determined my fifth-grade fate, had somehow stuck in my mind.

"Oh."

I chose a seat on the bus as far away from Patrick and chatty-red-dress girl as I could. A boy about my age sat next to me.

"Hey, are you new?"

"Yeah."

"What grade?"

He had to ask. "Fifth." I turned toward the window so I wouldn't have to see the surprised look on his face.

"No kidding. So am I."

I turned back to face him.

"Really?"

"I was sick a lot last year and missed so much school I have to do fifth over again."

"Really? What was wrong with you?"

"Cancer."

"Oh, man. What a bummer."

"Tell me about it. But…I'm good now. Feel great. Back in school. My name is Will."

"Ben. So tell me about this school. What should I know?"

We talked the rest of the way on the bus and walked into the school building together. Will went left to his homeroom class. I went right to the principal's office to receive my orientation and schedule.

* * *

"How did your first day of school go?" Mrs. Putnam asked. "I remember when our Phillip…"

I had learned to nod at all the appropriate moments. RULE 11: BE A GOOD LISTENER WHEN SOMEONE IS TALKING TO YOU. ACKNOWLEDGE WHAT THEY ARE SAYING. Apparently, the adults in the house didn't have to follow the rules.

"By the way, Benjamin, your aunt called today. She's coming home tomorrow."

"Really?"

"Oh, it's so nice to see you smile," she said. "You should smile more often. A smile takes fewer muscles than a frown, you know. I tell that to Patrick all the time too. Don't I, Patrick? They've actually done studies on it. In fact…"

I waited until the end of her speech before asking my question. RULE 4: DO NOT INTERRUPT ANYONE WHILE THEY ARE TALKING. Of all the rules, that was the hardest one to follow when Mrs. Putnam was talking.

"When can I go over there?" I asked.

"Over there? No, that wouldn't be allowed."

"Why not?"

"Don't raise your voice to me, young man."

RULE 1.

"I'm sorry. It's just that—"

"That's the second time you've broken that rule. You know the consequences if you break it a third time."

"Yes, ma'am." No TV for a week. I didn't care—I never watched TV with them anyway. I spent most of my time in my, or rather Phillip's, bedroom reading books he'd left behind. Luckily for me, there was no rule about books—a surprising oversight on Mrs. Putnam's part. At the time, I was immersed in *Jurassic Park*, a welcome escape from my own reality.

"The *Foster Care Handbook* says that family members may visit you here, supervised, but you can't go there."

"Supervised?"

"Yes. One of the foster parents has to be present during your visit."

I so wanted to know who had written up these rules, whose mission it had been to make it as difficult as possible for the foster kid. I wondered if all foster parents stuck as close to them as Mrs. Putnam.

"Could you arrange a visit with her as soon as possible, then?"

"Let's wait until she comes home. Then I'll contact Mrs. Brownback to discuss it with her, and we'll see."

*Geez, maybe we should also get this approved by President Clinton just to be on the safe side.*

"Yes, ma'am."

I never did answer her about my first day at school, which hadn't gone quite as badly as I'd expected. I still didn't want to be there—homeschooling was so much easier—but it was almost worth it to get away from Mrs. Putnam.

# Chapter 18

I came home from school the next day to find Aunt Birdie sitting at the kitchen table with Leah and Mrs. Putnam.

"Aunt Birdie!" I yelled as I ran over to give her a hug. As soon as I realized that I had just violated the no-yelling rule, I glanced over at Mrs. Putnam and mouthed "Sorry." I stayed as long as I could in my aunt's arms, even though she smelled a little like the antiseptic Mom used to use on us when we scraped a knee or something.

The first question I asked her was when Lucy and I could come live with her.

"Maybe the first thing to ask your aunt is how she's feeling," said Mrs. Putnam.

"How are you feeling, Aunt Birdie?"

"I'm feeling okay. The hospital stay took a lot out of me. But I'm getting better each day. Ben, I'm so sorry you're having to go through all this. Between your mother being… and losing your father, I…"

"Do you know where Lucy is?"

"I don't know *where* she is, just that she's in another foster home. I asked if I could visit her and was told it was too soon."

"Me too."

"I think it's going to be a while before I can take you in, dear. Because of my condition, CPS is requiring a medical report from my doctor to prove I'm physically able to care for you two, and he's not willing to do that yet."

She took my hand and told me everything was going to be okay, it would just take some time.

"How much time?" I asked.

"I have an appointment in six weeks. I'm hoping he'll sign off on it then."

I stared at the wall for the longest time, not sure what I wanted to do more—scream or cry.

"Can we talk every day until then? See each other once in a while?"

"Of course, sweetie. We'll stay in touch." She squeezed my hand. Her eyes filled with tears. "Your father was buried on the tenth. One day, we'll go to his grave together so we can say goodbye to him."

Before she left, I hugged her, long and hard.

"I hate it here," I whispered before I let her go. Looking back, I realize that was an unfair thing for me to say to her.

* * *

For the next several weeks, I struggled with school and was warned by my teachers that I had to maintain a C average in all my classes for the first report card in order to stay in fifth grade, and that except for reading and language arts, I wasn't likely going to make it. At the beginning of my sixth week in school, the principal called me into his office. Much to my surprise, Mrs. Putnam was sitting there with him.

"I think you may know why you're here, Benjamin," he said.

"My grades?"

He told me that at the rate I was going, I wasn't going to make it and suggested a tutor or a study partner.

Mrs. Putnam suggested Patrick.

My worst nightmare.

"Ugh…there's someone else who offered to help me, so I think I'll take him up on it."

"Oh? And who's that?"

"Will Jenner."

"He did?"

I rationalized breaking the no-lying rule by telling myself that I wasn't actually *in* the Putnams' home when I did it.

"When and where would you do that?" Mrs. Putnam asked.

"Well, we haven't exactly worked that out yet." That was technically true—the subject had never even come up between Will and me.

"Will is a very smart boy, and he'd be a good choice, but—"

"He doesn't live that far from us," I said.

"Would you like to work something out with Will's mother?" he asked Mrs. Putnam. "I suppose you should also involve Benjamin's social worker."

"But Patrick is just as smart, maybe even smarter, and he's right there," she said.

"I'd hate to hurt Will's feelings…"

After more discussion, Mrs. Putnam finally agreed, and before anyone could change their mind or contact Will's mother, I asked if I could go back to class.

When I reached the social studies room, the bell rang, signaling the end of class. I waited for Will to exit, grabbed his arm, and told him we had to talk.

"What did you do that for?" he asked after I explained. "We never talked about that."

"I know. And I'm sorry I lied like that, but they wanted me to work with Patrick and I freaked. I had to come up with something fast."

"Well, I don't mind helping you—these classes are a breeze for me—but how is this going to work if you can't leave the house without one of your foster parents?"

"I don't know. Can you make a pitch to your mom so she's on board when Mrs. Putnam calls her?"

"I'll try," he said.

When I got home that day, Mrs. Putnam had already spoken with Will's mother, who had said she'd talk to Will about it when he got home.

All I could do was hope for the best.

* * *

I used a calendar I'd picked up at school to keep track of important dates: the day Lucy and I left home, the day of my father's funeral, the day we entered foster care, and the most important one—Aunt Birdie's next doctor's appointment—November 2. That date I circled in red.

My social worker, Will's mother, the school principal, and Mrs. Putnam all agreed to allow Will and me to study together during our lunch break and after school, with Will's mother picking us up afterward and driving me home. I had until Christmas break to bring my grades up to a C in math, science, and social studies. Ten weeks to be able to add, subtract, and multiply fractions; list the properties of solids, liquids, and gasses; and understand what caused the War of 1812. Regular school was nothing like being homeschooled.

My jam-packed days left little time for feeling sorry for myself or worrying about Lucy. I got up early each morning to review what I had learned the day before, and after dinner each night I holed myself up in my room to finish homework. Will was a great tutor—so patient with me.

On the day of Aunt Birdie's doctor's appointment, Mrs. Putnam allowed me to call her—to place the call all by myself even. My excitement soon deflated when my aunt told me they'd found a tumor on her pancreas that had to be removed.

"When?"

"I go in on Friday."

"How long will you be in the hospital?"

"I didn't ask. I suppose it depends on what they find."

"Okay," was all I could think of to say.

* * *

Once I got the hang of things, Will and I were able to cut our study sessions in half, spending most of our time on math and science. Everything came easy to him. He explained it away by saying he'd been exposed to the same material the year before, but I didn't believe that. That kid was damn smart.

Once a month, Will came home from school with me. Rule 19: One same-sex friend is allowed to come over for up to two hours, no more than once a month. Rule 20: When a friend is in your bedroom, the door must remain open. I'm not sure what she thought might go on in there if the door was closed, or why someone coming over more often than once a month would be a bad thing. Questioning her rationale was pointless.

When Will did come over, we usually spent our two hours outside—on the patio, of course, where we were in plain sight at all times—even when the temperatures dipped below freezing. Before Will had gotten sick, he'd been taking karate classes and had worked himself up to a brown belt. His cancer prohibited him from continuing, but he showed me some of the moves, which I couldn't do very well. He talked about the mental side of karate, which I found interesting and, as I look back, helpful when it came to dealing with my emotions, which were often out of control.

If it hadn't been for Will, I don't know if I would have made it through the fifth grade, but it wasn't only because of his help with understanding the subjects. It was his friendship. I'd never had a best friend before, never knew the value of friendship. Connecting with someone my age who wanted to spend time with me made me feel good about myself.

Strangely enough, Will learned from me too. He kept asking me about my life at home, about the relationship I had with my parents, and the freedoms I enjoyed. I found out later that the reason for his interest was because he had been so overly protected by his parents his whole life—because of a variety of illnesses he'd had from the time he was born—that he longed to know what it was like for a kid to be able to fend for himself. I didn't understand his fascination at the time. Now I know that somewhere in the middle would be the ideal place to be for a kid.

When I told him about the trip I'd made in the Bronco, his face lit up, and he told me he could never have pulled off something like that. He looked up to me for it. Said I was his hero. That it took guts to do that, and skill, and courage—qualities he didn't have but wished he did.

The idea that anyone would wish they had what I had floored me. I didn't think I had anything.

# Chapter 19

The call I wanted so much to receive from Aunt Birdie finally came.

"I got it, Ben," she said. "A clean bill of health from the doctor."

"Really?"

"Really. But don't get too excited yet. You know I have to give this to CPS, and then it has to go before a judge, and then he or she will make the decision."

"Lucy too, right?"

"Yes, of course."

"I can't wait."

"Can I give you some advice, sweetie?"

"Sure."

"Try to hold your excitement down when you're in the Putnams' home. You wouldn't want them to think you can't wait to get away from them. Do you understand what I'm saying?"

"Yep. Got it."

I would have agreed to anything she asked.

* * *

Aunt Birdie's guardianship hearing was set for December 13. Arrangements had been made for all of us to meet beforehand in a private room at the courthouse—Lucy and me, our social workers, our foster moms, and Aunt Birdie. I hadn't seen Lucy in three months and was beside myself with worry but also excited at the prospect of seeing her.

Mrs. Putnam and I arrived first, followed by Aunt Birdie. I willed my heart to stop racing as I waited for the others to arrive. When the only ones left to arrive were Lucy and her social worker, I became so unnerved that I developed a facial tic I swore was keeping the same rhythm as the second hand on the large clock that hung on the wall.

Lucy's social worker, Mrs. Underbrink, entered the room alone. After taking her time removing her coat, scarf, and gloves, she joined us at the table.

"Where's Lucy?" I asked.

"She's not coming," she said, her hands in a prayer-like position on top of the table.

"Why not? Is she sick? Is she alright? What did they do to her?"

"No, no. She's fine. Um, Benjamin, Lucy is going to stay in her foster home."

"What?" I said in a loud voice.

"Benjamin, calm down," said Mrs. Putnam.

"That's my sister," I said in a tone I knew better than to use around Mrs. Putnam.

"She had a rough start," Mrs. Underbrink said, "but now she's doing so well, better than any of us could have hoped for, and none of us wants to disturb her. She and the twins have become fast friends. And she's doing very well in school too. She likes her school. Lucy is happy there."

"What about us?" I asked, referring to Aunt Birdie and me. "Didn't you tell her she could come live with us?"

"Of course, we did." She paused. "Normally, we don't allow young children to influence our decision as to what we feel is in their best interest. But in this case, Lucy has made such strides settling into a good, healthy family life, well, her opinion also counts for something." She turned toward Mrs. Brownback. "Here's what I propose. Go ahead with this hearing as planned, except take Lucy off the petition for now. The Larsens have invited all of you over to their home this coming weekend, so you can visit with Lucy, see where she lives, hear for yourself how she feels. We're supportive of the idea."

"This sucks."

"Benjamin," Mrs. Putnam whispered.

No one said anything for an uncomfortable several seconds. I didn't know if I was more angry or hurt. This couldn't have been Lucy's idea. She needed me.

"One thing I think we can agree on is that we want Lucy to be happy," said Aunt Birdie.

Everyone nodded, except for me.

"Ben?"

"Fine."

I didn't say anything more on the subject. What was the use? One stupid decision had just made our once-broken family beyond fixing. Or so I thought at the time. The numb feeling in my gut began to hurt.

The hearing lasted all of twenty minutes. I got the impression the judge had made up his mind before we even entered the room that he would grant my guardianship to Aunt Birdie. But what should have been a celebratory moment wasn't—I was too bummed out about Lucy.

Despite my mixed feelings toward Mrs. Putnam, it was still a sad moment when I said goodbye to her. I had lived in her home for three months and, all things considered, had been treated well. I told her I would come back the following weekend to say goodbye to Mr. Putnam. Patrick I would see in school.

Since Aunt Birdie didn't drive, Leah picked us up at the courthouse.

"Ben, I know you're upset about Lucy," Aunt Birdie said to me in the car. "But we have to keep her wishes in mind too, and if she's in a nice home and happy, well, that's a good thing, don't you think?"

"But I've taken care of her her whole life. What does that say about me?"

"It says you obviously did a good job."

"Yeah, right."

"She must have been a well-adapted little girl when she entered that foster home, thanks to you."

"I guess, but I still wish we were together."

"Let's see what we think after we visit her on Saturday."

I suddenly remembered my stash of things from the cellar.

"Oh, shit!"

"What?"

"I forgot something in my bedroom."

"Clothes? What? Homework?"

"We have to go there."

"That's way out of our way, Ben," Aunt Birdie said. "We can't ask Leah to drive all the way to the Putnams' and then back to my house. You can pick it up next weekend when you stop by there to say goodbye to Mr. Putnam."

"No. I have to get it now."

"What's so important?"

"Please?"

"What *is* it?"

"Just some of Mom and Dad's things. Can we please go back?"

"I don't mind, Birdie," Leah said.

When we arrived back at the Putnams', I was out of the car almost before it had stopped. Mrs. Putnam was surprised to see me.

"I forgot something in my room. Is it okay to go get it?"

"I'll get it for you. What did you forget?"

"Just some personal things that belonged to my parents. Private things I kept to remember them by."

I waited for her to step aside so I could run in and out with the shopping bag full of stuff that I had hid under my bed in preparation of my departure, but she didn't move.

"Stop fidgeting like that, Benjamin. What are you so nervous about?"

"Nervous? I'm not nervous. But Leah and Aunt Birdie *are* waiting for me, so I'd like to make this as quick as possible."

As soon as she gave me enough room, I scooted by her and did a fast-walk to my old room. Had it not been for Rule 23, I would have run. After I snatched the bag from under the bed, I turned around to face Mrs. Putnam and scurried past her.

"Thank you, Mrs. Putnam," I yelled when I was about halfway to the front door. "Have a nice Christmas!"

# Chapter 20

While Leah drove us to Lucy's foster home, Aunt Birdie told me more than once that I had to go there with an open mind and, above all, not try to persuade Lucy to come live with us. If she said she wanted to, that was different. But I wasn't to bring it up.

We arrived at noon. Leah said she would return to pick us up at three.

The Larsens' home was on a tree-lined cul-de-sac in Galena, not that far from Casey's General Store, which I avoided looking at as we passed. Their home wasn't any different from others in the neighborhood—relatively new, two stories, immaculately maintained, beautifully landscaped.

Mrs. Larsen answered the door.

"Come in, come in. We were—"

Before she could finish her sentence, Lucy came running out from behind her, screaming my name. She wrapped her arms around me with such force, I almost fell backwards. She looked different to me—taller, prettier…more put together.

"Luce—" I couldn't finish what I wanted to say—the lump in my throat wouldn't allow it.

"Well, let's get in out of the cold," said Mrs. Larsen, laughing. A slim woman with thick dark hair and exceptionally smooth skin, she reminded me more of someone you'd see on television than a mom.

With Lucy still holding on to me, I reached out to shake Mrs. Larsen's hand. "It's nice to meet you, Mrs. Larsen." I hadn't come up with that gesture on my own—Aunt Birdie had coached me beforehand.

"Oh, please call me Vet. Everybody does. Short for Yvette."

She led us into the living room and introduced us to her husband, Frank, and their twin daughters, Addison and Avery.

"Come see my room, Benny," Lucy said as she pulled on my arm. I glanced at Vet, who smiled in approval as Lucy dragged me up the stairs and down the hallway.

"Your hair," I said.

"What about it?"

"It looks so…nice."

"Vet does it for me. Even better than Mom."

I had to admit, it was a cool room—everything purple and white, unmistakably a girl's room. She opened the closet door. These are my new clothes…and shoes." She picked up a pair of black patent-leather shoes. "I never had shoes like this before."

"They're nice alright. Lucy—"

"Ben, I don't want to leave here. Vet and Frank are so nice, and so are the twins. I really like it here."

"I don't blame you, Luce," I said with conviction. "Your room is awesome. So is mine at Aunt Birdie's." My aunt's words of wisdom rang in my head. "You'll have to come see it sometime."

"Maybe you could come live here!"

"I don't think so. There's Aunt Birdie and—"

"Why not? They have lots of room."

"I know, but—"

"Don't you want to live with me?"

"Of course, I do, but I'm—"

"May I come in?" said Aunt Birdie. I hadn't seen her standing in the doorway.

"Aunt Birdie, what do you think of my room?"

"It's lovely. Isn't purple your favorite color?"

"Yep."

"Vet has lunch on the table, so you two come down soon, okay?" She winked at me and smiled.

"I hope she made shrimp," said Lucy. "That's my favorite."

"You hate seafood."

"Shrimp is not seafood."

"Yes, it is."

"It is? Well, I like it now," she said as she bounced down the stairs.

Three months had sure changed her.

I watched Lucy interact with her foster family during lunch, and while I hated to admit it, I couldn't find any fault with it. The twins talked about their friends and what they were going to do during their Christmas break. They included Lucy in the conversation like she was their sister. The parents treated her like she was one of the family. I studied Lucy's behavior—I'd never seen her so animated, talkative, and smiley. Gone was the shy, quiet little sister I had known with the permanently pouty face—the sister I'd taken care of and protected. Her new family suited her.

She didn't need me.

I continued to gaze at the happy family members wondering what it would be like to live with them until Aunt Birdie nudged me under the table and I made a conscious effort to stop staring.

On the way home, I told Aunt Birdie about Lucy wanting me to come live with her and the Larsens.

"Would you prefer to live there?" she asked.

"No, not at all," I said more convincingly than I felt inside. "But now I feel bad that Lucy thinks I don't want to live with her. I know how that feels."

"We'll keep in close touch with her—that's all we can do."

* * *

In the days that followed, I couldn't get Lucy out of my mind but kept reminding myself that the most important thing was that she was safe, well cared for, and happy. Still, it bummed me out that she seemed so well adjusted in the care of strangers. I confided in Will.

"I know what you mean," Will said. "When I was in the hospital last year, my sister came to visit me every day with my parents. And then it was every other day, and then once a week. Mom said she'd made some new friends in school and was doing different things with them. She told me I should be happy for her. But I didn't see it that way. I thought she didn't like me anymore. Didn't look up to me."

"Bummer."

"But then my mom explained that just because she had new friends didn't mean she thought less of me. She said the love she had for me came from a different place in her heart that no one else could touch."

"I guess I can see that," I said. What he'd said did make me feel better.

I could talk to Will like no other person I'd ever known. When something didn't make sense to me, whether it was school work or something personal, I knew I could go to him to try to sort things through. He was never hard-hearted or judgmental.

Will wasn't in school on the Monday of the last week before Christmas break. While we didn't have every class together, school wasn't the same without him. I missed him punching me in the arm as our paths crossed going from one class to another, pointing out cute girls, and eating lunch with me. At the end of the day, I called his home but got no answer.

The next day was report-card day, and Will was absent from school again. I wanted him to be around for moral support. Being in school that day was pure torture for me as I knew what would be waiting for me when I got home—I was not sure I'd be with the same classmates the following semester or put into the fourth grade, in which case I had already resolved to kill myself.

When I got home, I couldn't tell by my aunt's expression whether she had good or bad news for me. Finally, she looked at me with a glimmer of a smile and told me I'd passed every subject with at least a C. I tried not to let it dampen my spirits when she gave me her "I'll bet you could bring these grades up even higher if you worked at it" speech.

Later that evening, I called Will to see what was going on.

"I'm afraid he's in the hospital, Ben," his mother told me.

"Did he get hurt or something?"

She didn't say anything right away, and when she did speak, she did so with a shaky voice. "His cancer is back."

A few seconds ticked by before I realized the impact of her statement.

"He'll be okay, won't he?" I asked.

"I hope so, Ben. I hope so."

After we hung up, I told myself that, of course, he'd be okay. I'd seen people on TV all the time who had cancer and got through it—cancer survivor this and cancer survivor that. They had huge rallies about it. And Will had had it once and had come out of it. I was sure he'd be okay this time too.

Four days later, on the last day before Christmas break, I asked Aunt Birdie if I could go visit Will in the hospital. Before she asked Leah to drive us there, she called Will's mom to make sure that he could have visitors.

When she couldn't reach Will's mother, she called the hospital. "Only family can visit him, Ben," Aunt Birdie explained after ending her call. "He's in the ICU."

"What's the ICU?"

"Intensive Care Unit."

"Does that mean it's serious?"

"I'm afraid so."

"I want to see him."

"I know you do, but—"

"Can't you talk to someone? Isn't there—"

"Ben, rules are rules. You can't see him."

"I don't care about their friggin' rules. I—"

"Ben, I'm so sorry your friend is in the hospital and you can't see him, but there's nothing any of us can do about that. We don't always get what we want."

"Yeah, right. Like Will. Do you think he's getting what he wants right about now?"

I left the room, feeling bad about having taken it out on Aunt Birdie but not understanding why I had—maybe just because she was there.

* * *

Each day, until we heard from Will's mother in the afternoons, the hours dragged. I found myself watching the clock beginning after lunch, and when the phone rang, I would tense up watching Aunt Birdie take the call. I'd study her face to try to figure out his condition based on her expression. When she would say, "No change, then," I didn't know whether to be happy or sad. She ended every call with, "Tell him he's in our prayers, and we hope to see him real soon."

While it was nearly impossible to enjoy Christmas break from school with Will's life in jeopardy, I managed to get in two more visits with Lucy—one with Aunt Birdie and the other with just me. The time I spent with her new family reinforced the argument that Lucy was in a good place—Mr. and Mrs. Larsen made it easy for someone to feel part of the family, even me.

That got me to thinking about how dysfunctional my family had been—and about the lack of communication both between my parents and between them and me. When one of the twins asked Mr. Larsen why her aunt and uncle were getting a divorce, he took the time to explain relationships. My father would have told me to mind my own business.

Disheartening as it was, I eventually accepted the fact that Lucy was better off with them than with anything I could provide for her.

* * *

Two days before Christmas, my aunt and I were discussing the upcoming holiday when the phone interrupted our conversation. The pained look on Aunt Birdie's face as she listened to the caller on the other end scared me. She swiped at a tear as she hung up the phone.

"I'm so sorry, sweetie. Will didn't make it."

# Chapter 21

For days, I felt stuck in the moment when I learned of Will's death—nothing had prepared me for it. I knew he was very sick, but I thought he'd get better and be fine, like he had before, like other people had. It wasn't fair—not to him, his family, or me—and there was no one to complain to, no one to blame. I couldn't stop thinking that it could happen to any of us—to me, to Lucy, to Aunt Birdie. I hated thinking that, but it was true.

I spent the rest of that day in my room—crying, thinking of things I wished I had told him before he died, mad because I didn't have the chance to say goodbye to him. Even though I had known him for only a short time, our friendship ran deep. It really sucked, but his passing did wake me up about my relationship with Lucy. At least she was still around. Our separation seemed more tolerable.

At ten p.m., catching me in the middle of one of my crying jags, Aunt Birdie knocked on my door and asked if I needed anything or wanted to talk.

"No," I yawped into my pillow. "Just leave me alone."

She came in and sat down on the bed next to me.

"I'm not going to say I know what you're going through, Ben, because I don't. But I can tell you the pain is going to be with you for a while. Eventually, it will lessen and go away, but it takes time."

I turned to face her. "Why did it have to happen? I don't understand. He beat it before. Lousy doctors!"

"I doubt the doctors are to blame. It must have been in God's plan."

"Damn God, then. Why would He do that? Will never did anything to nobody. Why couldn't God take some bad person? Why did *he* have to die?"

"Cancer is a painful disease, Ben. We wouldn't have wanted Will to suffer with it, would we?"

"No, but why *him*?"

"I don't have an answer for that. I don't know that anyone does." She patted my leg. "I wish I could make you feel better, take the pain away, but I can't. Only time can do that. I'll tell you one thing I do know for sure—Will is going to be with you for the rest of your life…in spirit. And I think he was lucky to have you as a friend."

After she left my room, I cried again. And once I started, I couldn't stop. For a reason I didn't understand then, I was more upset about Will's death than about my own father's. Now I understand that in some ways I was closer to Will than to Dad.

* * *

Leah had invited us to her house for Christmas Eve dinner. Also invited had been Leah's sister and niece. Aunt Birdie told me she had been going to Leah's on Christmas Eve for years but that if I didn't feel up to it, she would understand and stay home with me.

Aunt Birdie also left it up to me what we would do on Christmas Day. We'd been invited to the Larsens'. The other choice she gave me was to stay home and have a quiet day together, which meant for me focusing on Will's death and spending more time alone in my room.

Making decisions at this time had become difficult for me, even small ones. I told her I didn't care what we did.

"Then, let's go to Leah's. Keeping busy will help you take your mind off Will, even if just for a few hours."

"That doesn't seem right."

"Why do you say that?"

"It would be wrong for me to forget about him."

"I didn't say forget about him. You'll never forget about him, and you shouldn't. What I'm saying is—"

"I'm staying home. You go to Leah's."

"A minute ago, you said you didn't care what we did. I guess you do care."

"I don't know!" I yelled at her before stomping to my room.

It took me a while to realize how stupid it was for me to treat my aunt that way. She had nothing to do with Will's death. I apologized and said I thought we should go to Leah's for Christmas Eve and Lucy's for Christmas Day.

"Good," she said. "I think Will would have wanted you to do that. He wouldn't want you to be sad 24/7, right?"

"Probably not."

"Ben?"

"What?"

"You're a good kid, you know that?"

"Yeah, right."

She smiled. "Most of the time."

I smiled back. "You just had to add that, didn't you?"

* * *

Will's mother called us on Christmas Eve morning and asked if she could come over. My stomach, which had finally calmed down a bit, now churned more than ever in anticipation of why she wanted to talk to us. She arrived with an envelope in her hand.

"I was going through Will's things in preparation for his funeral on Thursday when I found this." She handed me a sealed envelope with my name on it.

I froze—seeing my name in his handwriting caused a sudden coldness to surge through my body.

"Should I open it?" I asked.

Will's mother turned to Aunt Birdie, who shrugged.

"If you want. Or save it for later. I don't know what's in there."

I stroked the envelope—why, I don't know. To buy some time perhaps. Or maybe knowing Will had once held it gave me comfort or strength or something. I slid my finger under the flap and removed the piece of paper inside. After I read the first few lines, I smiled.

"I don't know if you're going to think this is funny or not, Mrs. Jenner, but whenever we were in Will's room, and you had the TV on, it was usually tuned to the same program."

She hesitated a moment before responding. "Not *Golden Girls*."

"That's the one. And it got so we knew most of the lyrics to that theme song, and we would sing along, really soft so you wouldn't hear us, acting silly doing it and everything."

"I can picture you two stinkers doing that," she said. "I'll get you guys for making fun of my TV shows." After she'd said it, she teared up.

"So what's on the piece of paper, Ben?" Aunt Birdie asked.

"The complete lyrics. I don't know where he got them because we had to skip through some parts we didn't get."

I glanced down at the bottom of the page where Will had written:

*Read the last stanza. You and me, kid.*

I read it and then let the paper drop to the floor as I pushed myself up from the sofa and ran to my room, bawling like a baby.

*And when we die and float away*
*Into the night, the Milky Way*
*You'll hear me call, as we ascend*
*I'll see you there, then once again—*
*Thank you for being my friend.*

# Chapter 22

I tried to psyche myself up for Christmas Eve dinner. Leah's sister and her sister's niece would be there—three middle-aged ladies, whoever the niece was, and me. "Deck the halls" and all that fun stuff.

Aunt Birdie and I were eating breakfast that morning when the phone rang. After hanging up with the caller, she said, "Sheriff Joe is coming over in an hour to talk to you."

"What about?" By then, I had come to believe his interrogations of me were history.

"He didn't say, and I didn't ask. If it was something he could have discussed on the phone, I figured he would have."

That piece of news did nothing for my sensitive stomach. It couldn't be about the Bronco—calling it "abandoned," he'd had that towed in September, as promised. Something about my mother maybe?

I stayed in my room until the sheriff arrived, at which time the three of us sat at the kitchen table.

"I'd like to know, Ben, if you recognize anyone in these photographs." He spread out head shots of six different men in front of me.

Melvin was second from the end. I tried not to stare at him too long.

"No," I said, shaking my head.

"You're sure?"

I glanced at them again. "Mm-hm."

"What's this all about, Sheriff?" Aunt Birdie asked.

He fixed his gaze on me as he answered her question. "One of these gentlemen may have some connection with the items stolen from Abigale

Washington's home, that's all."

"May I ask what that has to do with Ben?"

"His mother used to work for the late Mrs. Washington."

"She died?"

"Yes, ma'am."

"How does any of this involve Ben?"

"No stone can be left unturned in an investigation, ma'am. Just doing my job." He got up to leave. "Merry Christmas," he said halfway out the door.

I couldn't imagine how Melvin fit into all of this. Could it be that Melvin and my mom knew each other? That maybe his being at that general store the night the Bronco broke down wasn't just by coincidence? Sheriff Joe seemed like the kind of guy who was going to get to the bottom of it one way or another, and that scared me.

"Do you have any idea what that was all about?" my aunt asked.

"Not a clue."

I hated lying—it caused stress. I needed less stress, not more.

A few hours before we were to leave for Leah's house, I was so disturbed by the number of unanswered questions concerning my mother that I considered telling Aunt Birdie I wasn't feeling well and wanted to stay home. Before making that decision, I told her I needed to go the library real quick and look up something for school.

"The library is open today?" she asked.

"Until 2:00."

"Okay."

The local library was within walking distance. When I arrived, I told the reference desk librarian what I was looking for. She found an article on microfilm that said on September 6, the police had confiscated a bag of "objets d'art" found in the Honda Accord my father had been driving when he crashed into a parked vehicle. *September 6 was the day my father left us home alone to pick up Mom at work.* The items were later identified as having been stolen from the residence of the late Mrs. Abigale Washington, who had employed my mother as her caregiver. My mother was arrested and charged with grand theft. Mrs. Washington's gardener was charged with second-degree murder. *She was murdered?* But he pled "not guilty."

I reread the article, more slowly this time. Did my mother know the gardener? Did she know he had killed Mrs. Washington? And how did

Melvin fit into the picture? It was sounding more and more like a mystery novel by the minute.

I looked up the term *objet d'art* and learned it was an object of artistic worth or curiosity, especially a small object.

Like all the curious-looking things I had stashed in the suitcase.

*Shit.*

I left the library overwhelmed and confused and was glad to find Aunt Birdie with her coat on when I arrived home—distracting me from fretting over it further.

"Are you ready, Ben?"

"Yep."

We walked around the corner to Leah's house.

"In nice weather, we walk to each other's houses through the backyards," Aunt Birdie explained. "They actually butt up against each other." That explained why Leah had gone to Aunt Birdie's back door when she discovered Lucy and me huddled on her patio. Good thing she did, or we may not have been discovered until way later.

When we got there, Leah introduced me to her sister, Claudette, and Claudette's niece, Georgia.

"Hey, I think I know you," I said to Georgia. She wasn't at all what I expected—she was close to my age.

"You look familiar too. Do you go to East Dubuque?"

"Yeah."

"Who do you have for math?"

"Bensueller."

"Second period?"

"Yep."

"We're in the same class," she said.

Leah's house had been decorated for Christmas more than any house I'd ever seen—with a giant Christmas tree, candles burning, a nativity scene on the mantle, garlands and bows everywhere, and a fire in the fireplace. All Aunt Birdie had in her house was a twelve-inch tabletop Christmas tree and a snow-globe that played "White Christmas" if you wound it up. Even my parents' house had at least been graced by a beat-up fake Christmas tree Mom had retrieved from Mrs. Washington's garbage. Aunt Birdie said she just didn't have the energy to decorate this year. I offered to do it for her, but she said she didn't even have the energy to think about it.

After dinner, we all sat in the living room to talk. The Christmas music playing in the background made me feel like I was on a Christmas TV special, causing me to wonder if more people lived like this than like the way I had.

The four females did most of the talking. I sat there and listened with half my mind. The other half was on the stash I had in the suitcase, the sheriff's visit earlier in the day, and the fact that Mrs. Washington was murdered on the same day my mother and possibly my father had been at her house. My dead father. My dead, probably drunk father.

I became vaguely aware of Georgia saying something that might have been addressed to me.

"Did you say something?" I asked.

"You seem to be in some other place," she whispered.

She had a nice smile. I had never paid any attention to her in math class. Being extremely shy around girls, I had never paid much attention to any of the girls in my classes. That smile. I felt like such a dope not having listened to what she'd said. I hoped she didn't think I was a total bonehead.

"I asked where you went to school last year," she said.

"I was homeschooled."

"Really? That's awesome."

"Not so much. They placed me in fifth grade here instead of seventh."

"How old are you?"

"Twelve, but please don't tell anyone. I feel bad enough as it is. How old are you?"

"Eleven. I didn't go to kindergarten until I was six, so I'm a year older than everyone else too."

"So how are you related to Leah?"

"My Aunt Claudette's late husband was my mom's brother, and Aunt Claudette and Leah are sisters."

"Okay. I think I've got that. So where are your parents?"

"Both are out of town, so that's why I came here."

"Got it."

"You knew Will Jenner, didn't you?" she asked.

"He was my best friend."

"I'm so sorry. He was awfully nice."

"I know."

"Are you going to the funeral?"

"Yeah, I'll be there."

"Maybe I'll go too. I know a lot of kids from school are going."

"Where are many kids going?" her aunt asked her.

"Will's funeral."

"I'm driving Ben and Birdie there," Leah said. "I could pick you up on our way."

"That would be great."

So now it looked like Georgia and I were going to a funeral together.

* * *

Aunt Birdie and I had bought a Christmas present for Lucy and a little something for each of the Larsens. As we wrapped the gifts on Christmas morning, I got to thinking about Will's funeral.

"Do you think it would be okay if I read the words to that song on Mrs. Jenner's TV program at his funeral, the ones Will wrote out for me?" I asked her.

"Really? You want to do that?"

"Kind of dumb, huh?"

"Not at all. I was just thinking you'd be standing in front of a lot of people, at an emotional time, and…"

"I want to do it."

"We'll need to ask his mother."

"Could you call her?"

"Sure. When I get back from church."

"I bought a little something for the Putnams for Christmas," I told her.

She smiled and patted me on the hand. "What a thoughtful idea. We can drop if off later today if you want."

With Aunt Birdie at church, I took the opportunity to drag the suitcase from underneath my bed and retrieve the baggies full of what I hoped hadn't been stolen by my mother from Mrs. Washington's house. She had already been charged with grand theft—would adding to the stuff she stole be cause for a more serious charge?

"Artistic worth or curiosity," it had said in the dictionary. I picked up one of the ivory figurines and studied the intertwined arms and legs of two naked people. It certainly fell under the category of "curious."

Before I'd realized that these items had possibly been stolen, I'd considered wrapping the sparkly Hello Kitty figurine and giving it to Lucy for Christmas, since she liked it so much. But not now. Curious as to its worth, I searched for it in the bag. It wasn't there.

I reflected back to when I'd last seen it. Lucy had pulled it out of the suitcase when we were stuck in Casey's parking lot. I remembered being upset because Melvin was standing nearby, and I didn't want him or anyone else to see what we had. Later, when we were at Melvin's, I saw the figurine in the suitcase, but it was not in the baggie I had originally wrapped it in. I figured I had probably shoved it into the suitcase in the parking lot and hadn't bothered to put it back in the baggie.

Melvin was the only person who could have gotten into the suitcase—when I was sleeping or in the bathroom. Or, I supposed, Mrs. Putnam could have taken it when I was at school. I quickly scratched her off the list of possible suspects—stealing was against house rules—and concluded Melvin must have taken it.

# Chapter 23

Mr. Larsen picked up Aunt Birdie and me for our holiday visit. As much as I was still upset with Lucy for choosing to stay in her foster home, I had to admit that the Larsen situation was pretty damn good—nice house and car, both parents easy to talk to, girls close to her own age, and Lucy had things she'd never had before. Why wouldn't she choose them over me?

"So are you a Cubs fan, Ben?" he asked me in the car.

"You bet."

"I have season tickets for home games, if you're interested in going sometime."

"Are you kidding? I'd love it!"

Of course, that gave me another reason to like him.

Lucy greeted me with a big hug as soon as I walked into the house, which reeked of scented candles.

"Merry Christmas!" she squealed in an excited, high-pitched voice I had never heard come out of her before. "Look at all these presents," she said pointing to the tree, quashing any lingering resentment I still harbored toward her for abandoning me.

"I see."

She pointed to a pink two-wheeled bike. "Look what I got."

"A two-wheeler, Luce? You've never ridden one of those."

"Vet is going to teach me when it gets warmer. It's brand new too." We never got brand-new anything at home.

"Awesome."

We all sat down in the living room around the Christmas tree and opened gifts to the strains of holiday music playing through high-end speakers. My favorite gift, one I still have to this day, came from Lucy—a thermal mug, the kind where you can insert your own design under the clear plastic outer shell.

To my best bruther
in the hol wide world
Love, Lucy

It was in her handwriting. I made some silly remark to cover up my real emotions.

* * *

The day after Christmas, I ran to the library and found my favorite reference librarian to ask her to help me find information on two of the "objets d'art." She was able to find a collector's book on all sorts of Hello Kitty items as well as a few articles on microfilm that included how much some of them sold at auction. I paged through the book and scrolled through the articles until I found something that resembled the now missing figurine. Under the auction photo, it said OPENING BID $100,000. I knew that couldn't be right, so I kept scrolling.

Nothing else looked similar, so I stopped the Hello Kitty search and focused on the purse with the shiny stones. By now, I had watched the librarian enough to do it on my own. I was about to give it up when I found the exact purse listed for $1.63 million. Made out of platinum and encrusted with 2,013 diamonds totaling 195 carats, it was described as "a very expensive handbag."

The one in the article listed the designer as Ginza Tanaka of Japan. Its authenticity had been verified by the label sewn inside. Mine had no label. I searched for articles on fake Ginza Tanaka handbags and found a *Forbes* article that showed a picture of a similar bag worth $85,000.

The last thing I did was ask the librarian, who now called me her favorite patron, where I could find Whiteside County court records. She referred me to the county courthouse in Morrison. For now, I had to tuck that information in the back of my mind as I had to get home before Aunt Birdie returned from shopping with Leah.

118

* * *

I woke up on Thursday morning, the day of Will's funeral, sweating. The horrible feeling in my chest made me want to put my head under the covers and go back to sleep…for the rest of the day. At that moment, I considered it the worst day of my life and decided I must have been out of my mind to offer to read the "Thank You for Being a Friend" lyrics during the service.

When we picked up Georgia for the funeral, she told me she was nervous, saying it was her first funeral.

"Mine too," I said.

"I thought you said your dad died."

"He did, but I didn't go to the funeral. I don't know if there even was one." I glanced at her. Her unblinking eyes remained wide for several seconds. "Long story."

"Well, you look very nice," she whispered.

"You too," I said, thinking afterward that that was a lame response.

The packed church emitted a buzz of soft, low voices. Just as we were about to sit in one of the back pews, Will's mother came up to me and asked me if I would sit up front with them. I glanced over at Aunt Birdie with what I suspect was a look of panic. She gave me one of those you-can-do-this nods, and I followed Mrs. Jenner to the first row. I was taken aback by the sight in front of me—the closed casket draped with Will's brown-belt karate outfit. At the same moment, I was handed a program with Will's face on the cover.

Sitting myself down next to Mrs. Jenner, I opened the program and saw my name listed under "Time of Remembrance," right after the names of his mother and father. I checked my pocket for the millionth time to make sure I had the sheet of paper containing the lyrics with me.

The minister opened with a prayer intended for Will's parents. Even though his Mom leaned on her husband to her left, I could still feel her body trembling on my side. Guessing what they were going through made me realize that my nerves likely paled in comparison.

We stood and sang "Amazing Grace," and then the minister read from the Bible—something about someone's father's house having many rooms—followed by another prayer. I didn't understand any of it. When it was time for Will's mom and dad to speak, they walked hand-in-hand up to the pulpit.

Will's mom started by talking about the day Will was born, six weeks too soon with resulting complications. After describing his first day at school, she talked about his earliest serious illness—a rare form of brain cancer—and how they went through treatments for a year until the glorious day when they were told it was in remission. She talked about their feeling of helplessness when they learned it had come back with a vengeance.

Will's dad talked about how rewarding it had been for him to watch Will grow into a fine young man who had talked about becoming a fireman one day.

His mother finished by saying that not only had Will been a loving son, but he had also been a loving friend to many. "His best friend, Ben Mattis, would like to say a few words," she said. "And while Ben is making his way up here, I have to tell you that what he is going to read to you is going to be a testament to what TV show I often watch in my spare time. And it's okay to laugh at me. Laughter is good."

By the time I reached the stage, my legs shook so badly that I feared they might fail me altogether. I thanked God—someone I had never spoken to before—for the pulpit, the edge of which I grabbed with both hands to steady myself.

"Okay, here goes. First, I need to say that Will and I used to lip-synch to this song whenever Mrs. Jenner watched… I never remember the name of the show, but I think most of you will know it after I start reading."

I made it through most of the lyrics without stammering or stuttering too much. After I read the first two or three stanzas, I could tell by the tittering in the audience that they knew the television show. When I reached the last stanza, I began tearing up. But I didn't care, I blubbered my way through it. Will's mother stood behind me and held on to my shoulders until I finished.

I knew I would never forget that day—reading those lyrics was the hardest thing I'd ever done. I've had to face some extremely difficult things in my life, more than the average Joe, but none as emotionally taxing as this.

But I knew Will appreciated it, and that made it all worthwhile.

# Chapter 24

The ride home from Will's funeral was quiet, except for when Georgia put her hand on my leg and said, "You did *so* good up there. I would have just *died.*" When she teared up, I fished from my pocket a handkerchief Aunt Birdie had given me and handed it to her.

*Thank you, Aunt Birdie.*

Will's mom had invited us back to their house after the service, but I declined for all of us, thinking they probably hadn't counted on four of us, and if the gushing about my performance after the service was any indication of how I would be treated in their home, well, I'd had quite enough. I did feel proud of myself for getting up there and letting my emotions hang out like that. But it wasn't something I wanted to do again any time soon.

Georgia's mother Theresa invited us over to eat lunch, and we accepted.

She and her mom lived in an impressive ranch home a few blocks from Aunt Birdie's. When we got there, we settled into their family room. Georgia's mom lit a fire in the fireplace with a flip of a switch—something I'd never seen before—and then turned on Christmas music by remote control. I tried to curtail my amazement.

After pizza had been ordered, Georgia told her mom she was going to show me the rest of their house.

The downstairs was nothing like I'd ever seen before. Seating for at least a dozen people surrounded a huge TV screen. A second TV screen for gaming hung on the wall on the opposite end of the long, narrow room. Off to the side was a bar and Ping-Pong table that faced a massive fireplace. The far end of the room was comprised of floor-to-ceiling windows with doors leading out to a patio and an endless wooded backyard.

"How big is your family?" I asked.

"It's just Mom and me now. My parents were divorced last year."

"Sorry to hear that. Where's your dad?"

"Colorado," she said and then paused. "Living with a girl ten years older than me."

"Oh."

"I shouldn't have said it that way."

"That's okay." I didn't know what else to say. "Do you get to see him often?"

"I haven't seen him since he left." She rolled her eyes. "He called on my birthday."

She went to the phone, pressed a couple of buttons, and said, "We're going to stay down here until the pizza comes. Is that okay?"

I must have had a bewildered look on my face.

"Intercom system," she said after her mother acknowledged her message. "Beats yelling."

We sat down on the sectional but didn't turn on the TV.

"Does your mom work?" I asked.

"She's a patent attorney."

"Really? What does a patent attorney do?"

"She works with inventors mostly, helps them get a patent on whatever it is they invented. She does a lot of pro bono work too."

"Pro *what-o* work?"

"Pro bono. She works for free."

"Why would she do that?"

"If a client is under eighteen or over sixty-five, she usually helps them for free."

"Cool."

"And she also teaches a patent law class at the community college."

"Your mom sounds smart."

"Yeah, I guess so."

"What does your dad do?"

"He's an attorney too. Corporate law. Nothing like Mom."

"Why did they get divorced?"

Without equivocation, she said, "Because my mom's a lesbian."

I knew what lesbians were but had never actually known one. That said, Georgia's mom looked like an average mom to me, so maybe I did know some and didn't realize it.

The arrival of the pizza prevented me from asking any more questions.

* * *

There was so much more I wanted to know about Georgia and her family, and that opportunity presented itself the following Tuesday in math class on our first day back at school after Christmas break.

"When do you get lunch?" I asked her after class.

"Noon."

"Do you want to eat together?"

"Sure."

"Meet you there, then. Let's try to get that table in the corner by the windows."

"Got it."

My next two classes were a complete blur. Georgia was one of the prettiest girls in my class, and knowing that several of our classmates had overheard our conversation about having lunch together gave me a much-needed ego boost. While I tried to focus on homophones and idioms in language arts class and the Mexican-American war in history class, my mind kept drifting to black-haired, blue-eyed Georgia.

"Hey," I said to Georgia in the lunch line.

"Hey, yourself."

Standing in the lunch line, I was faced with a big decision—order my usual burger and fries or eat healthy to impress her. It would have been an easier decision had she been in front of me to set the example. My eyes darted to the healthy selections—turkey wrap, vegetable lasagna, and a variety of salads.

"Turkey wrap, please," I told the cafeteria lady behind the counter. She gave me a surprised look—in my small school, the ladies behind the counter knew our preferences. She glanced at Georgia and smiled. She knew.

"That sounds good," Georgia said. "I'll have the same."

I led the way to the table in the far corner of the room, feeling good about my food decision.

"So what's your next class?" I asked her.

"Language arts." She made a face.

"You don't like it?"

"It's my hardest subject."

"That's funny—it's my easiest."

"If I need help sometime, could I call you?"

She could have called me in the middle of the night to ask me to explain the difference between infinitive and auxiliary verbs, and I'd have been cool with it.

"Sure."

We talked about our other classes and spring break.

"We're going to Cancun," she said. "We have a timeshare there."

"A timeshare?"

"A condo that we share with a bunch of other people, not at the same time though. We also go there for ten days between Christmas and New Year's. Although, we didn't go last year. My mom's partner had her appendix removed in December."

"Partner? Like in a law firm?"

"No, her significant other."

This was so new to me. I took an extra big bite of my wrap so I'd be busy chewing while I pondered what she'd said.

"If this is making you uncomfortable, just let me know. I'm used to it."

"No, not at all," I mumbled as I tried to swallow a huge mouthful of food.

"Tell me about your parents," she said.

She had been forthcoming with me, so I decided to be the same with her.

"I have a little sister who's in a really nice foster home. My mother's in jail for grand theft, and, well, you already know my father is dead."

Her eyes went wide. "Your mother is in jail?"

I smiled. "If this is making you uncomfortable, just let me know. I'm used to it."

She held up her hand for a high-five. "You crack me up," she said. She glanced at the clock on the wall and then quickly rose from her chair. "Gotta go. My locker is clear on the other side of the building from my next class. Call me?"

She was gone before I could respond.

It took me several seconds to recall what class I had next.

# Chapter 25

I didn't like the fact that I was being kept in the dark about my mother. I was almost thirteen—old enough to understand adult things, so I thought. I wanted to know if there was any hope of being together as a family again, and if so, when. I was done living day-by-day. I wanted a plan. I was also getting tired of getting from place to place by asking Aunt Birdie, who in turn had to ask Leah to drive us—I went from being almost independent to relying on others for everything. I made my feelings known to Aunt Birdie one Saturday as I helped her clean the house.

"How far is the county courthouse from here?" I asked her.

She stopped dusting the bookshelves and turned to me. "Why on earth do you want to know that?"

"I want them to show me my mother's sentencing hearing so I can see how long she's going to be in jail."

"Why?"

"Because I want to know."

She went on with her dusting.

"So you're not going to tell me?"

"Sit down, Ben."

By the solemn look on her face, I knew she was about to tell me bad news.

"I don't want you to worry about that. Concentrate on kid things—like homework, and having fun, and that crush you have on Georgia."

"I don't have a crush on her!" I said as the warmth rose up my neck and into my face.

"Mm-hm."

"You're trying to change the subject."

She laughed. "I know, and it almost worked."

"I'm old enough to know. Do you know?"

She didn't respond.

"Aunt Birdie?"

"Yes, I know."

"Tell me."

She stared at me for a brief time before responding. "She was sentenced to five years."

"Really?"

"My understanding is that the judge could have given her fifteen years, but since the stolen items were recovered, he went with the minimum sentence."

"Do you know where she is?"

"She's in Decatur Correctional Center."

"Where's that?"

"Near Springfield."

"Why all the way down there?"

"I don't know."

"Do you know that Mrs. Washington was murdered?" I asked her.

"I know someone was charged with her death. He hasn't been to trial yet. I think he too was charged with grand theft. That's what one newspaper article said."

I didn't know that the gardener had been charged with grand theft.

"So they both stole from Mrs. Washington?" I asked.

"Looks like it."

"Together?"

"That I don't know."

"How did my dad fit into all of this?"

"All I know is that a sack of stolen items was found in the trunk of the car he was driving when he had the accident."

"Was my mom in the car with him when it happened?"

"I don't know."

"Do you still have the newspaper articles?"

"You don't want to—"

"I can find them at the library."

She sighed. She was good at staring off into space when she didn't want to answer something.

"Okay. I'll get them for you when we're finished cleaning. When you're done reading them, I want them back."

"No problem. Aunt Birdie?"

"What?"

"There's something else on my mind."

"What's that?"

"Do you think I could get a bike this spring? You know, so I can go places by myself."

"Like where?"

"You know, the store, the library…"

"Georgia's house."

"Aunt Birdie."

"Sorry, couldn't help it. I know how it feels to depend on others to get around. When I lost…"

"Lost what?"

"Nothing. Not important." She hesitated, and for a moment, I thought she was going to tell me something personal. "How about if you earn it?" she asked.

"What do you mean?"

"I hadn't thought about it before, but you should be getting an allowance for what you do around here, like Saturday morning cleaning and taking care of Paws. And then if you do something above and beyond, like help me clean the basement or the garage, I'll give you extra."

"How much?"

"How much do other kids get?"

"I have no idea."

"We'll come up with something."

* * *

Depending on the exact month she was released, I figured I'd be either sixteen or seventeen when Mom got out of jail. With any luck, I'd be a junior in high school, at least a sophomore, but only a freshman if I continued to advance at the snaillike pace I was currently going. It was a difficult scenario to envision—Mom coming home and the three of us living together again after her absence of five years. I chose not to think about it.

The articles about my parents that Aunt Birdie had collected revealed two interesting things. My father's middle initial was *M.* I didn't know that. And his blood-alcohol level at the time of the accident was 0.2—more than twice the legal limit.

I had not thought my father was drunk when he'd left our house that day to pick up our mom—although sometimes it was hard to tell with him. I remembered it being in the morning. I reread the articles to see if they listed a time of day for the car accident. It had happened at three-thirty in the afternoon. I scanned the article for when they found Mrs. Washington—that had been the following morning.

Even with this additional information, what had happened wasn't clear to me. I wanted to know if Mom was in the car when Dad crashed it. Or if there was any connection between her and the gardener accused of killing Mrs. Washington.

Another big unknown was whether Melvin had any connection with either of my parents or the missing Hello Kitty figurine. And perhaps more significantly, what was the sheriff's theory about the connection between Melvin and me? My guess was that he had questioned Lucy and she had given him enough information to raise some suspicions.

I hadn't heard from the sheriff in a couple of weeks, and that made me nervous.

# Chapter 26

What had started out as a frightening, unwelcome experience—going to public school—turned out to be something I preferred over being homeschooled. At first, I found the discipline unnerving—I was used to working at my own pace at home, taking breaks whenever I wanted—but once I got accustomed to the new system, I understood why kids my age were two grades ahead of me. And after a while, I found myself craving to learn more. I loved the learning process—something I'd not felt being homeschooled.

Being around so many other kids scared me at first—I wasn't used to such different personalities and diversity—and seeing them interact with each other in so many different ways got some getting used to. I know now that between being homeschooled and my parents not being social people caused me to become somewhat introverted, and that staying home with just my sister to interact with was a lonely way to live. School was a place for making friends.

And it took me a long time to realize the value of teachers, as my first impression of them was that all they did was make my life difficult. But that changed over time. When I was being homeschooled, I didn't get much help if I had a question about a certain subject or a homework problem. Mom was usually too tired, angry, or disgusted with Mrs. Washington when she came home from work. And forget about asking my dad—he either didn't know or was passed out on the living room sofa by the end of the day. Having a teacher to answer questions was great.

And then there was basketball. My school had a basketball team comprised of sixth-, seventh-, and eighth-graders. Will had encouraged me to try out.

"But I'm only in fifth," I'd told him.

"I know, but you're twelve. You qualify with your age."

"But I never played."

"With your height, you'll be a natural."

I was accepted on the team, and not only did I love playing, but I slimmed down a few pounds in the process. One game, I was even the high scorer. Aunt Birdie must have been proud of me because she slipped an extra five into my allowance that week, bringing my savings up enough to buy a used bike.

Toward the end of the school year, I asked my favorite teacher, Mrs. Forde, what I could do to catch up so I could eventually graduate from eighth grade with kids my own age. She told me she was willing to put together a lesson plan for me to follow the entire summer that would prepare me for placement testing before the new school year started—they would use that to determine if I went into the sixth grade or the seventh. If I could go directly into seventh grade, I'd graduate middle school with kids only a year younger than me.

Georgia and I sat together on the bus to and from school when I didn't have basketball practice and continued to meet each other for lunch every day. In my mind, and in the minds of the kids who were into gossip, we were boyfriend and girlfriend. But I wasn't so sure what Georgia thought—I learned that it wasn't easy to know what girls thought most of the time, and since I was so self-conscious around her, I didn't have the wherewithal to feel her out. I wanted us to be more than just friends, but I didn't have the nerve to make the necessary moves. Outside of school, we hung out, helped each other with homework, and talked. She shared with me things about her childhood and family that were unfamiliar to me, like fun vacations and large family get-togethers, and while my life experiences seemed hardly worth sharing, I did the same with her.

I still had Lucy on my mind, usually when I was trying to fall asleep at night, but not quite as much anymore. It helped me to remind myself that she was in a good place, a safe place.

* * *

The day after school let out for the summer, I bought a bike. With all the time I spent riding over to Georgia's, helping Aunt Birdie with things around the house, attending summer basketball camp, on top of the four hours a day it took to follow Mrs. Forde's lesson plan, it was a busy summer.

My birthday was July 4. Based on the date, one might have thought my birthday celebrations had always been fun-filled and exciting. Not so. My mother's birthday was July 1, and we had always celebrated our birthdays together—or, more accurately, *not* celebrated our birthdays together. Mom hated birthdays. The most we ever did was stick a couple of candles in an ice cream jelly roll and call it a day. But this year was different.

For my birthday, Aunt Birdie invited Lucy and her foster family over for lunch. After eating a casual meal, Aunt Birdie brought out a birthday cake that read "Happy 13th birthday, Ben. Now go clean your room!"

When I opened Aunt Birdie's gift, I let out a scream.

"Are you kidding me?" A bedroom-size TV with a built-in VCR.

"There will be rules," she warned.

I didn't care about rules. I figured all the kids in my class had TVs in their rooms, but I assumed it was out of the question for me.

From the minute she walked through our door, Lucy seemed a little quiet to me, so when I got her alone later I asked her if everything was okay.

"Sure," she said. "Well, no. Maybe not *all* okay."

"What's going on, Luce?"

"I just miss you, that's all."

"Come here, you little… Hey, you're not so little anymore." I gave her a hug. "I miss you too." I released her from my grip and looked straight at her. "You still like it there?"

She nodded.

"Because if you're not happy there, I'll—"

"No, I'm really happy there. I just wish you were there too."

"I know, but I need to stay here with Aunt Birdie. She needs me."

"So do I, Benny."

"But you have the Larsens. Aunt Birdie doesn't have anybody. Do you understand that?"

"I guess so."

I hoped she did understand. When they were getting ready to leave, Lucy hugged me and whispered, "I think you should stay here with Aunt Birdie." That made me feel better, a little less guilty.

Georgia had invited me over after dinner, saying she had "a little something" for me. The "little something" turned out to be not so little—she'd invited all the boys from my basketball team to watch *Ferris Bueller's Day Off*—a movie I had seen on TV so many times I knew most of the lines. It turned out I wasn't the only one obsessed with the movie. When I asked Georgia how she'd pulled that off, she told me her mom was friends with the coach's wife, and they had done all the planning, making me feel pretty special.

I sensed a swell in my chest as I biked home, and despite the night chill, warmth throughout my body. Before I walked into Aunt Birdie's house, I had to make a conscious effort to curtail the ridiculously big smile that had been plastered on my face all evening—it was so awesome to have Georgia as a friend.

# Chapter 27

Mrs. Forde's lesson plan paid off, and I was allowed to enter the seventh grade at age thirteen. It was a rigorous schedule with checklists to follow, recommended books to read over and above my school textbooks, and periodic check-ins with her to make sure I was keeping on track. Determined to not disappoint Mrs. Forde and myself, I kept to it, wearing earbuds at home to keep distractions down, limiting fun stuff, and asking for help whenever I needed it.

Fifth grade had been rough, but seventh grade was even worse—coming into it behind the other students was a clear disadvantage. But I persevered and managed to end the school year with a C average.

By eighth grade, I was on a relatively even playing field with the other students, and looking back, I'm pretty proud of that. What I'm not so proud of is that toward the end of the year, I became lax in my studies, spent too much time goofing around, and didn't graduate. I had to make up U.S. History in summer school and retake the Algebra final to get my middle-school diploma.

Aunt Birdie was disappointed in me, but not as disappointed as I was with myself. As nervous as I was to enter high school, I vowed to do better.

* * *

There was no denying that Lucy was thriving with the Larsens. When I thought back to the girl she'd been when we left home that fateful night three years earlier, there was no comparison, and we owed it all to the

Larsen family. Lucy and I saw each other on holidays and a few times in between when I'd be invited over for a birthday party or barbecue or some other event, like going to a Cubs game. And Aunt Birdie was in frequent contact with Mrs. Larsen as well. Lucy was happy, and I was happy for her.

Aunt Birdie's health continued to improve, and as it did, so did her extracurricular activities. Together, she and Leah participated in book clubs, church events, and their favorite activity—bingo. Unfortunately, something else changed in Birdie coinciding with her improved health—moodiness. Sometimes I may have caused it—like cranking up the music in my bedroom too high—but other times it seemed to come on unprovoked. In addition, her memory wasn't always that good and I thought she could do with a hearing aid. But I had it good there—better than any foster home, I believed—so I tried not to let it get to me.

My relationship with Georgia vacillated between just friends and something more. The ambiguity was difficult. Part of me felt it was safer to keep our relationship platonic. The other part of me was driven by hormones, I suspect. I felt like I had no control over which way it went, and so I allowed the relationship to be governed by the one with the more dominant personality—Georgia.

* * *

I was scared to death to enter high school. Georgia, one grade behind me, wouldn't be there to be my lunch buddy, my confidant, my best friend. Somehow, I made it through the first week.

On the Friday afternoon at the end of that week, Georgia's mom picked us up at our respective schools and dropped us off at the mall, saying she would come get us a couple of hours later. At the mall, Georgia took me on a stroll through the lingerie store Victoria's Secret. Embarrassed by the array of bras, thongs, and some undergarments I couldn't even identify, I felt like I couldn't get out of there fast enough. She didn't buy anything and appeared to be amused by my reaction to her holding up one garment after another to ask for my opinion. Fun for her, apparently, but not for me. I was in some ways rather immature for my fifteen years, not much of a seducer or even a seducee.

Afterward, we bought sodas and sat at the edge of the food court to people-watch.

At first, I didn't see him approaching. It was his familiar voice that got my attention.

"Hey, kid!" Melvin said, still several feet away.

"Who is that?" Georgia asked under her breath.

I didn't respond to either of them. Instead, I froze.

"You didn't tell me that stuff was hot."

Before he could get any closer, I got up from my chair to face him.

"Not here, Melvin."

He grabbed my arm and led me away from the food court.

I turned around to face Georgia—her mouth was wide open.

"I'll be right back," I said to her.

Melvin and I stopped when we reached the railing overlooking the first floor of the mall. I hoped he hadn't noticed my shakiness.

"You got me into some deep shit, kid. Spent ninety days in jail because of you. You know what I'm talking about," he said.

"Uh, no."

"Does Hello Kitty ring any bells?"

"Kind of."

"Don't lie to me, smartass. You knew that stuff you carried in your suitcase that you guarded with your life was stolen. Admit it."

"I didn't then."

"Right."

"How'd *you* get it?"

"Spotted it by the side of the road is what I told the cops. Sun was shining right on it, like a deer in headlights. Finders keepers and all that shit. But I got caught trying to pawn it. Turns out it came from some rich bitch's house in Galena, but something tells me I don't have to tell you that."

"I didn't know that."

"Then?"

"Now, even."

"So how'd you get all that stuff?"

"I'd rather not say."

I glanced at Georgia, who had a scared look on her face.

"I'll bet you don't. I could have gotten up to five years for that. And what about that murdered woman? I'm surprised they didn't question me on that too!"

"You had nothing to do with that…did you?"

"Shit, no. You know how much that piece of crap cat is worth?"

I shook my head.

"I was told over fifty grand."

"I don't believe it."

"Well, believe it, dumbass. Those red, white, and blue stones were diamonds, rubies, and sapphires, as if you didn't know. If I'd pulled that off, I'd have been set for life…a thousand miles away from Nurse Ratched."

"I didn't know. I swear."

"Right. You're lucky I'm the kind of guy I am and didn't turn you in."

"I didn't turn you in either."

"What are you talking about?"

"The sheriff wanted to know where I was for those two days we were at your house. I didn't tell him anything about you."

"That right?"

"And when they showed me your mug shot, I said I didn't recognize you."

"Well, you're lucky you didn't."

"Can I ask you something?"

"Shoot."

"How did the Bronco get back on the street by my aunt's house?"

"Dick and I fixed it and put it there for you. How do you think it got there?"

"Thanks."

He waved me off. "Go back to your girlfriend, kid."

I walked back to Georgia on wobbly legs.

"Who was that?" she asked. "I didn't know if I should call my mom or the police or find someone here to help you. Who *was* that?"

I took in a deep breath. "It's a long story."

"What did he mean when he said you didn't tell him the stuff was hot?"

"He was just kidding."

"He looked like he was really pissed off."

"That's just his way. He wasn't pissed."

"He reminded me of the Joker from *Batman*."

"He's not that bad."

"How do you know him? Is he a friend of yours?"

"Friend of the family." Georgia was the last person I wanted to lie to, but she left me no other choice.

"I don't know, Ben. He creeped me out."

When it was time to meet Georgia's mom, we walked down the long corridor to the mall entrance. Halfway there, I took her hand, only to have her take it back. The first time I'd felt brave enough to make a move, and she rejected it. I didn't know why she did—either she didn't want her mother to see us holding hands, she was upset over Melvin, or she preferred to be the initiator. I could drive myself crazy trying to figure it out, so I didn't.

# Chapter 28

I managed to get through my freshman year with a C- average. But instead of having coursework, Georgia, and basketball on my mind most of the time, I spent much of the schoolyear worrying about the stash of stolen items I had hidden in Aunt Birdie's attic. I worried about how much more trouble my mother would be in if the authorities knew she had stolen them and how much trouble I'd be in if they knew I'd been harboring them all this time—or even worse yet, if my aunt was now somehow culpable having them on her premises.

One Sunday morning during summer break, when my aunt was at church, I studied the items again: the fancy handbag, eleven jade animal figures, eight ivory-carved people and animals in embarrassing poses, the lamp with the boy leaning against a lamppost, a gold locket, and a letter signed by George Washington. I examined the locket—the portrait on the front of it could have been George Washington, but I wasn't sure. After fingering it for a while, I realized it opened—inside was a portrait of a woman in a really ugly hat. I put it back and placed one of the ivory pieces in my pocket.

I needed to know how much the stuff I was harboring was worth, so I left for the library for another laborious search. I didn't know what to call the ivory figurines. I started by looking for books and articles on figurines in general. That too broad a category, I tried for "naked figurines." The words "shunga netsuke" were mentioned in many of the articles, so I looked up that term.

> Shunga netsuke: a form of netsuke art where sexual connotations are
> freely represented in figural and symbolic forms.

After a lengthy search for netsuke art, I found a picture of one similar to the one in my pocket. This one had sold for $225, but the article said age played a major role in putting a value on these figurines. If each of the ones I had was worth $225, that would be a total of $1,800.

Aunt Birdie was due home soon, so I stopped my search and went home. The other items would have to wait.

* * *

Now old enough to get a work permit, I applied for a summer job as a stock boy at a local grocery store. Come July 4, I'd be sixteen and old enough to drive. I had taken driver's education in school and had done pretty well—learning a lot of things that would have come in handy when I drove from Fulton to Galena almost four years earlier. Aunt Birdie promised that when I had half the money required to buy a car, she would put in the other half, as long as I promised to take her places so she wouldn't have to rely on Leah so much.

One day after I got my license, Leah and Aunt Birdie took me car shopping at a local used-car lot. The sleazy salesman who waited on us must have taken us for pushovers to buy whatever he recommended. We may have been naïve, but we weren't idiots. We left without buying anything.

I didn't know anyone who could help me buy a car, at least not one that needed careful scrutiny and cost under a thousand dollars. I remembered Melvin's friend Dick, who seemed to know all about cars, and wished I knew how to get in touch with him. I couldn't remember the name painted on the side of his tow truck, so I checked the Yellow Pages for tow truck companies in Jo Daviess County to see if anything would jog my memory. Shocked at how many towing companies serviced our area, I scanned the list for a familiar-sounding name. None stuck out except for Irish Rover Auto Service, not because of the name but because I remembered a four-leaf clover on the door of his truck. I took a chance and called.

"May I speak with Dick?"

"Dick here. What can I do for you?"

"You may not remember me. You towed my father's white Bronco from Casey's when I—"

"Oh, I remember you alright. Wondered what happened to you over the years, kid." His bullfrog voice was unmistakable.

I didn't know how to interpret his remark, whether it had a positive or negative undertone.

"Anyway, I'm old enough to drive now, and I'm looking for a car, something under a thousand dollars, and I thought maybe you'd know of something."

"What happened to the Bronco?"

"The sheriff had it towed somewhere. I didn't have any registration for it. It may have been stolen. Thanks for fixing it though."

"No problem. If I remember correctly, Melvin paid for the parts. Look, I don't know of any decent cars for under a grand, but if you give me a phone number, I'll call you if I run across something."

"I'd really appreciate that." I gave him my number, and we ended the call.

* * *

The summer between my freshman and sophomore years whizzed by—my only regret being that I didn't have much time to spend with Georgia. Between my work and taking a summer sociology class, and her dance classes and involvement in her mother's office, our schedules rarely had openings at the same time. I looked forward to the fall when we'd be in the same school. Until then, we talked briefly almost every day.

I still didn't know what Georgia really thought about me. She could be flirtatious, but most of the time what she said could be taken more than one way, so I didn't respond in kind. I had it so bad for her, but I didn't want to jeopardize what we had or make a complete fool of myself. If she had a real boyfriend, she hid it well from me. I secretly hoped all boys were as ignorant as I was when it came to girls. I didn't want to be the only one.

The week before school started, Dick called me to say he knew someone who bought cars cheap, fixed them up, and resold them.

"He's got three right now. A 1990 Ford Fiesta with 50,000 miles on it. A 1992 Toyota Camry with about the same mileage. And an '83 Mustang convertible, 86,000 miles but a real cool car. If you're interested, I'll go over there with you, make sure you're getting what you pay for. Kind of like to see that Mustang myself."

He agreed to pick me up the following Saturday.

When I told Aunt Birdie about it, I cringed when she said she'd come with. Here I was acting all grown up about buying a car, and I had to bring my aunt with me—my aunt who didn't drive and probably didn't even know the difference between automatic and manual transmission. But she was putting up half the money, so what could I say?

Saturday morning, Aunt Birdie received a call from someone in her church asking her if she could fill in for a woman who'd cancelled at the last minute for their bake sale. Saved.

"Don't worry, Aunt Birdie," I told her. "I'll get something you won't be embarrassed to have parked in your driveway, something you'll be comfortable in."

"Okay, dear. I'm trusting you."

Judging by the look on her face, I didn't think she did.

"I'll stop by the bake sale to give you a lift home in my new car, if it works out."

"No hot-rodding!"

"Huh?"

"Drive carefully."

"Yes, Aunt Birdie."

# Chapter 29

Dick picked me up in his tow truck, the same one he had used to drop me off at Aunt Birdie's almost four years earlier.

"Hey, kid, hop in."

We talked about cars on the way there—mostly, he was advising me on what to consider in a used car. He told me about his first car.

"It was a 1943 Buick Roadmaster I inherited from my uncle when he died. Maroon with white leather seats. What a car. V-8 engine, Dynaflow torque converter transmission. Had that baby up to 100 mph once. Wish I still had it—be worth a fortune today."

"What happened to it?"

"Totaled it, driving drunk. Lucky to be here." He paused. "I did my share of stupid things back in the day. Don't you do the same."

"You're talking to the twelve-year-old who drove forty miles in the middle of the night in a broken vehicle with no registration, no plates…"

"Yeah, well, I hope you learned your lesson."

"Yep. Sure did."

The man with the cars for sale had them lined up in his side yard for us to view. My gaze went right to the Mustang—yellow with a black convertible top. I pictured myself driving to school in it. Aunt Birdie in the passenger seat, not so much. I walked closer to it—even I could tell that it needed a lot of work.

"Body is not in such good shape, but it runs well," the man said.

I joined Dick standing next to the Toyota Camry, whose body was in much better shape. Dick started it up and then opened the hood to observe the running engine. After he asked the guy a few questions about the car, he got permission to take it for a spin.

Dick drove. "This isn't a bad little car," he said after we had gone a mile or so down the long, winding road. "Handles okay, doesn't pull to the left or right, good pickup, brakes." He sped up—way over the 35-mph speed limit. "Shifts okay." He slowed down before he pulled off to the side of the road. "You drive it back."

The only previous times I had driven a car were in my driver's ed class, the day I took my driver's test, and of course the night I drove the Bronco when I was twelve. I adjusted the seat, buckled up, and checked all the mirrors before I took off.

"Ha! Driver's Ed 101," he said. "You did say you have your license, didn't you?"

I laughed. "Don't worry. I have it."

On the way back, Dick told me what to look for in the interior of the vehicle, which I did while he talked price with the owner.

After I finished checking the inside, I joined the two of them.

"I got him down to $875. What do you think?" he asked me.

I glanced at the Mustang.

"It's got 86,000 miles on it, needs new tires, and the top won't last many more winters," he said.

I didn't like what he'd said, but I knew he was right and that I shouldn't consider it. There went my vision of being cool man on campus.

"And the other one?" I asked.

"That one needs new tires too, and I don't like the corroded tailpipe. If it's acid causing it, there could be hidden problems." He walked over to the Camry. "You'd be getting a good car with this one."

As hard as it was to be practical at a time like this, I had to go with his recommendation—he knew what he was talking about.

Before I drove off in my new car, I pulled Dick aside to talk to him.

"By any chance, do you remember how much Melvin had to pay for those Bronco car parts back then?"

"Under a hundred bucks, I think. Not sure of the exact amount."

I pulled out my wallet and handed him five twenties, leaving the remainder of my car fund at twenty-five dollars. It didn't bother me that Melvin might have stolen some of my stuff—he had still helped me out of a jam. "Will you give him this? He shouldn't have had to pay for it."

Dick peeled off three of the twenties and handed them back to me. "Just give him forty bucks. Won't hurt the son-of-a-bitch to be a little charitable once in a while."

* * *

I never thought I'd feel so good on a first day of school—I was now a sophomore—but driving my own car did that for me, and it didn't hurt to have Georgia in the passenger seat beside me.

"Mom wasn't going to let me ride with you at first, you know," she said.

"Why not?"

"I think just the idea of me being in a car with a boy freaked her out."

"Ha! She knows me. I'm relatively harmless."

"And that's the only reason she let me—she likes you."

"Well, I'm glad somebody does."

"I like you."

This was what confused me about Georgia. She'd say something like that, and I didn't know if she meant it literally, as in "I like you as a friend, nothing more," or if she liked me as in boyfriend, or if she was just fishing for me to say something about my feelings for her. How do you know what a girl means when she says, "I like you"? I didn't know then, and I still don't know.

"Yeah? So tell me, what do you like about me?"

"Well…you have good hair."

"Gee, thanks a lot. That's all you can come up with?"

"No, I can come up with a lot more, but I wouldn't want to give you a swelled head or anything."

"I see. How about if you give me just one a day?"

"Only if you do the same," she said.

"Deal."

"Deal."

"When is your lunch period?"

"Eleven-forty-five."

"Crap. Mine is twelve-thirty."

"Your first class?"

"Chemistry. Yours?"

"Language arts."

On the way to our first class, we talked about where we'd meet up after school. But my mind wasn't on chemistry—not the academic kind anyway.

# Chapter 30

Four years had passed since my mom had gone to prison, and I still hadn't spoken to her, not even once, although I could have. She called Aunt Birdie occasionally, and each time she did she'd asked if she could talk to me. Each time I'd said no. I wasn't sure what I was afraid of—something in my head just said not to give her that satisfaction. The longer she was away, out of my life, the stronger I felt about not talking to her.

At Aunt Birdie's urging, she and I had discussed my establishing some kind of relationship with Mom during her incarceration. Visits were out of the question—my aunt didn't think that a prison environment was any place for a kid. At that age, I thought it would have been cool to see the inside of a prison, but that still didn't make me want to see her.

Mom had written me several letters that I'd read and shared with Aunt Birdie. Even if I had wanted to respond, I wouldn't have known how. Mom had a way of saying things that made me want to turn a blind eye. How do you respond to someone who says, "Tell me how your life would be different if I'd never gone to prison?" Why would I spend my time even thinking about that?

But Mom was supposed to be released in a year, barring any unforeseen circumstances, and I suspected the first place she'd come would be Aunt Birdie's. In the back of my mind, I knew I had to start preparing myself for her return as that time grew closer.

I was home alone on a Saturday in early November. Aunt Birdie was at bingo with Leah. I had called Georgia asking her if she wanted to come over and hang out for a while. She rode her bike over.

As she walked in the door, she uttered just one word. "Forgiving."

"Understanding," I said.

We had been giving each other one-word things we liked about each other daily since the first day of the school year. I didn't know about her, but I was running out of adjectives that didn't skirt the romantic boundaries.

That day, we talked mostly about school while watching *Footloose,* a movie from the eighties we both loved.

A half hour into it, the doorbell rang. Thinking my aunt was home and had forgotten her key, I swung the door open, ready to greet her.

But it wasn't Aunt Birdie. I didn't know who it was until she called me Benji. Only one person had ever called me that.

"Mother?" I'd never called her that in my entire life.

"Look at you! Come here, sweetie," she said taking a step closer to me and holding her arms out.

She didn't look the same. This woman was shorter than the one I remembered. But then it just seemed that way because I had grown taller. Her thin body I remembered had grown thick and soft. And her hair, once blond and coiffed, was now brown and pulled back in a ponytail. She didn't even sound the way I remembered her. And she smelled funny.

Her bark-like cough snapped me back to the present. I backed away.

"Come in…I guess," I said. When I turned around, Georgia was in front of me.

"Is it your aunt?" she asked.

I shook my head.

"Who is it?"

My mother walked past me and held out her hand for Georgia to shake.

"I'm his mother. Who are you?" She turned to me. "You have a girl-friend, sweetie?"

"Yes, I'm Georgia," she said shaking my mother's hand.

*Yes, she's my girlfriend?*

I struggled for the right words.

"Um…we didn't exactly expect you…"

"I got released early," she said walking past both of us. "Good behavior. Are you surprised?"

Georgia and I stared at each other, mouths agape.

"I should go," Georgia said.

"Please don't go. I'm not prepared for this," I whispered.

"Where did she go?" Georgia asked.

We followed the sound of my mom's coughing to the living room where we found her sitting on the sofa flipping through an issue of *Newsweek*.

"Where's Birdie?" she asked.

"At bingo. Was she expecting you?" I asked.

"We talked about it—my coming here to live until I got back on my feet."

"You talked about it?" Aunt Birdie had never said anything to me.

"Well, maybe we never did finalize it, but…"

"I really should go, Ben."

"You don't have to leave on my account," my mother said without glancing up from the magazine.

Georgia shot me a pained look.

"Okay. I'll walk you to the door," I said.

Once we were outside, I closed the door.

"I'm sorry, Ben, but I don't think I should be here. This is between you and your mom."

"I know. I wish I had known she was coming. I don't even know what to say to her. And now she's going to live with us?"

Georgia leaned in and kissed me on the lips.

"Good luck," she said.

Before I knew what hit me, she was on her bike and riding down the driveway.

I touched my lips. Georgia had kissed me. I started to sweat like I'd just run a lap around the outdoor high school track in the hot sun. I wanted to sprint after her, go in for a second one. The last thing I wanted to do was ruin the moment by going inside and facing my mother, but I had no choice.

I glanced at the kitchen clock as I passed through—four-thirty. Aunt Birdie usually arrived home around five after bingo. I had a million questions for my mother, but I thought it might be better to ask them with Aunt Birdie present. Scared, but wanting to be brave, I raised my head, straightened my posture, and joined my mother in the living room.

"Nice girl," she said.

"Mm-hm," I said, Georgia's kiss still lingering on my lips.

"How long have you two been dating? Can't be too long, being you're only fifteen and all."

"I'm sixteen."

"Sixteen? Must have lost a year in there. How's your sister?"

"She's fine."

"You know, the first thing I'm going to do is go to court to get custody of you two."

That was enough to send tremors through my body.

"Lucy is very happy where she is."

"In foster care? I don't think so."

"I've been to her home. It's really nice. And her foster parents are great."

"So you see her often?"

"Yep. And we talk in between visits."

She made a face. "Really."

"Really."

"Well, that's all well and good, but you know what they say—there's no place like home."

"But you don't have a home." The moment I said it, I knew I shouldn't have.

"I will, son. As soon as—"

She stopped talking when Aunt Birdie walked into the room. I hadn't heard her come in. She didn't say anything to either of us—just stared at my mother for a long moment—and when Mom made no effort to rise up to greet her, then plopped down into her easy chair.

"Long time, no see, eh, Birdie?"

"I wasn't expecting you until next year," she said. "How are you, Rose?"

"Can't complain."

"You got out early?"

"They cut my sentence for good behavior." She smiled, and that's when I noticed she had a tooth missing, near the front. "I was an outstanding prisoner."

"You should have told us," Aunt Birdie said. "We would have arranged to pick you up."

"I wanted it to be a surprise, and—"

"How did you get here?"

"Took a bus as far as Chicago, then a Metra train to some podunk town not that far from here. Some nice kid I met on the train dropped me off here."

"What happened to your tooth?" I asked.

"Which one?"

"The missing one."

"Just a little chin check, that's all. Happens all the time in prison. No biggie."

Neither Aunt Birdie nor I reacted to her statements. I couldn't speak for Birdie, but I didn't know how to react.

"So, Birdie," she said. "We talked about my staying here for a bit, just until I can get my shit together and a place of my own."

"I don't remember that conversation, Rose, but—"

"Yeah, well, we did. Your memory isn't what it used to be, eh? So what do you say? Can you help a girl out? Pay back a favor? I know you have the room. And then I'd be back with my boy."

"You're completely free and clear?" she asked.

"Almost. Five years' probation. It's nothing."

"What can't you do for five years?" she asked.

"Can't be employed in someone's home. That's all."

"What kind of job will you be looking for, then?"

My aunt asked good questions—better than I could have come up with.

"I'll find something. Hey, I just walked in the door. Give me some time to recover from that hell hole."

My mom was in no position to be a mother. Even at my age, of that I was sure. She had no place to go, no money, and she seemed lost. But I did like the fact that now I could get the entire story about what had happened the day she left Lucy and me to fend for ourselves.

* * *

While driving Aunt Birdie to church the morning after Mom's arrival, I asked her what she thought about Mom's surprise appearance. It seemed to me that she had been holding back what she really thought.

"I don't know, Ben. On one hand, regardless of what she did to get herself in there, now she has no place to go, and I have to feel sorry for her. But I don't like the way she just popped in without calling first and taking it for granted that I'd let her stay."

"Can I ask you something?"

"Go ahead."

"How did you get along with my parents before?"

"Okay."

"I mean, were you and Dad close?"

"Once upon a time, before…"

"Before what?"

"Before you were born."

"What changed?"

"A lot of things, Ben. Adult things."

"You're not going to tell me, are you?"

"No. It's history."

"So what are you going to do about Mom?"

"I don't know."

She was clamming up on me, and I didn't like it when she did that.

"Tell me what Dad was like before I was born."

"He was a good man, Ben. He helped me through some tough times. Both your mom and dad did. Mostly your mom."

"What kind of tough times?"

We reached the church parking lot, and when I stopped to let her out, she remained seated, staring past me for the longest time.

"I'm an alcoholic, Ben," she said without looking at me.

"What?"

"I've been sober for almost fifteen years, but I'll always be an alcoholic."

"I didn't know that."

"I know. Not many people do. Not something I'm proud of."

"Mom and Dad helped you get sober?"

"More than that. They put up with my irresponsible behavior for years. Always stuck by me no matter what I did. DUIs, public drunkenness, on the brink of bankruptcy. They were there for me through all of it."

I couldn't picture my Aunt Birdie drunk.

"What happened fifteen years ago?" I asked.

"I got drunk and drove, without a license. That would have been my fourth DUI…had it not been for your mother."

"How so?"

I crashed the car into a tree, taking down three mailboxes in the process."

"Where was this?"

"In front of your parents' house. Your mom came running down the drive to see what all the commotion was, found me, unconscious outside of the car, and called 9-1-1. I came to before they arrived, and she told me to tell them that she, your mother, had been driving and swerved to miss hitting a dog."

"And they believed it?"

"I guess so—she wasn't charged with anything."

"So that's what she meant by paying back a favor?"

"Probably."

After hearing that story, my opinion of my mother changed, not a whole lot, but some.

When I returned home, I caught my mom walking out of my bedroom.

"What were you doing in there?" I asked.

"Look Monkey Mouth, I'm still your mother, and don't you forget it. I can damn well go in your room if I want to. Capisce?"

"Monkey Mouth?"

"Prison expression. Don't worry about it."

I said nothing as I walked past her. She followed me into my room.

"So how'd you get that big chip on your shoulder, son? You don't see me for four years, and this is how I'm treated? What happened to you while I was gone?"

I swung around to face her. "What happened to me? You're a few years late in asking that question, don't you think? What do you think happened to me?"

"For your information, I know what happened to you—I've kept in touch with Birdie."

"Why'd you ask then?"

"What I meant was—"

"You want to know how it feels to be twelve years old and abandoned by your parents, wondering what was wrong with you that would make a parent do that?"

"It wasn't like that, Ben. I didn't abandon you. I—"

"Well, that's what it felt like. You want to know what it's like to have a six-year-old sitting on your lap so scared that she pees all over you? You want to know what it's like to—"

"Ben, I'd like to explain—"

I rushed past her. "I'm outta here."

* * *

I hated my mother for showing up. Just when things seemed to be going well for me, she entered the picture and stirred everything up again.

I drove to Georgia's. She met me at the front door.

"What's wrong? Your call scared me."

I threw my hands in the air. "I wish she'd never shown up!" I regretted not having simmered down before coming over. I didn't want Georgia to see me so out of control.

"Your mother?"

"She's nothing but a goddamn ex-con looking for a frickin' handout."

Her mother walked into the room.

"I'm sorry, Mrs. Franzen, for using that kind of language, but—"

"What's the matter, Ben? I've never seen you like this."

"It's my mother, I—"

"Georgia told me she came home."

"It's not *her* home!" I stopped to calm myself down. "I'm sorry. I'm sorry."

She took my arm and led me into their living room. "Let's sit down and talk this through. Would that help?"

For the next hour and a half, the three of us talked—mostly I did the talking. Getting it all out helped. When I was done, I told Georgia's mom I didn't know how I could possibly be nice to her given what she had done, regardless of how she had helped save Aunt Birdie's neck that time.

"I think it's important for you to know everything that happened to her after she left you and your sister alone, and for her to know everything that happened to the two of you. But unless you both do it in a calm, loving way, it may do more harm than good."

"I don't know if that's possible. I can't even look at her for too long without feeling like I'm going to puke."

"She's only been home…sorry, in your aunt's home, for less than twenty-four hours and—"

"Exactly, and that's all it's taken to disrupt our lives."

"What I was going to say is that maybe you two need to get to know each other first—you're not the same people you were four years ago, not by a long shot. That will give you time to understand each other better. Does that make sense?"

"It makes perfect sense…when you say it. Doing it is another story."

"I know. Just remember to always take the high road. That's something no one ever regrets."

I left their house feeling a lot better. Georgia was so lucky to have a mother like that.

# Chapter 31

When I arrived home after the talk with Georgia's mom, my mother was in her bedroom with the door closed. I didn't expect my aunt home from church until later, as she had planned to participate in something following the service. I went into my room, closed the door, and began a list of questions I had for my mom, a second list of things I wanted her to know about what went on while she was gone, and a third list of things I didn't want her to know about what went on while she was gone. I wasn't sure when we would have such a discussion, but I wanted to be ready for it when we did. She had claimed she knew everything we went through via her discussions with Aunt Birdie, but she didn't. How could she? Aunt Birdie didn't know the half of it.

As soon as I heard the knock on my door, I slipped the list under my pillow.

"Can I come in?" she asked in a restrained voice I almost didn't recognize.

"Sure."

She opened the door. I could tell she'd been crying. She sat down on my bed, her limp clasped hands resting in her lap.

"I'm sorry I came here assuming I'd be welcomed with open arms. That was foolish on my part."

I didn't know what she expected me to say—*That's alright, mommy, dear, all is forgiven*?

"Okay."

"You learn to keep your defenses up when you're in prison." She looked down, like she was searching for the right words. "It was horrible in there.

Sharing a nine-by-twelve-foot cage with three other delinquents and never turning your back on them in fear of what they might do to you. Working twelve hours a day in a hot, steamy laundry room for fifty cents, breathing in who-knows-what kind of chemicals. Or cleaning toilets, earning enough to buy toothpaste, soap, and an occasional candy bar. Just when you feel you're at the lowest point ever in your life, the guards harass, humiliate, or abuse you to beat you down even further."

I wanted to say, "Well, you have no one to blame but yourself for being in there." But I didn't.

"You cough a lot."

"Kennel cough. It'll go away."

"You just compared yourself to a dog."

"Yeah, well, maybe that's how I've been treated for the last four years—like a dog, an abused dog."

I knew she wanted me to feel sorry for her, show some compassion. Maybe I should have, but I just didn't have it in me.

"So what's your plan?"

"Plan for what?"

"For your life. What are you going to do for a job? Where are you going to live?" I sounded more like a parent than she did. I resented her for that.

"Ben, you don't just get out of prison and slip into a comfortable life. It doesn't work that way. And it's not going to be easy finding a job with a criminal record—I'm forbidden to work as a caregiver, which is the only job I ever had."

"I thought they offered classes in prison so people could land a job when they got out."

"That only happens in the movies."

"You need some kind of plan."

"Look, kid, I'm still the parent here."

"I work part-time and go to school full-time. After I finish high school, I plan to go to a community college and get a degree. Maybe I'll get married someday. Have a family. I don't have it all worked out yet, but at least I have a plan."

"You think you know it all, don't you?"

"I learned a lot about life after you and Dad abandoned us." I regretted those words as soon as I said them, but the tension that was building up inside wrung it out of me.

She got up, and before leaving my room said, "Your dad is dead. At least show *him* a little respect."

* * *

The next several days must have been rough on my aunt. She never said anything to me that would have indicated that, but there were signs—the pinched expression on her face, the periodic strain in her voice, moodiness. One day, as I drove her home from a hair appointment, I asked her if she was feeling okay.

"I'm okay, Ben. Not sleeping very well lately. That's all."

"It's Mom, isn't it?"

"No, I—"

"I know it's her. Even when she's not saying or doing anything, she can be irritating. And then when she does open her mouth, I have to hold back from saying what I really want to say. Don't you feel that way too?"

"You're being pretty hard on her, don't you think?"

"Do you know that she's been here almost a week and hasn't asked me what happened to us after they left?"

"Maybe she's afraid to hear it. Feels guilty about it."

"Maybe she needs to own up to it. And she hasn't done a damn thing about getting back on her feet."

"Ben, your language."

"It's true. She's such a slacker, and we're tiptoeing around her and waiting on her hand and foot like she can't do anything for herself."

"Maybe she can't."

"Right."

"She's been told what to do and how to do it for the last four years."

"Well, maybe she needs to snap out of it. Does CPS know she's living here?"

"Yes, I informed them."

"Did they have a problem with it?" I could only hope.

"No. They said that since you're sixteen, the court gave her unlimited visitation rights with you."

"What about Lucy—same thing?"

"In her case, a court-approved supervisor would have to be assigned."

"Does Mom know this?"

"Yes."

"I wish she wasn't here."

"She has no place to go, Ben."

"That's not *my* fault."

"I know it isn't, but we can't just kick her out into the street."

"Why not?"

"Ben."

"She can go to a shelter. I'm sure there are some around here, and if there aren't, I'll drive her to one—the farther away the better."

She let me think about what I'd said for the remainder of the drive home. Before I got out of the car, she touched my arm.

"It's my house, Ben. I still make all the decisions."

* * *

Trying my hardest to follow the advice from Georgia's mom about taking the high road, I decided to ask Mom in the most positive way I could about what happened on that fateful day that led up to her going to jail. To create alone time with her, I offered to drive her to Chicago to a place with a reentry program for ex-offenders—coaching, mentoring, counseling, job networking—everything I figured she needed to be on her own. The fact that I was the one who had found this place didn't give me much confidence that it would do any good. Still, I thought it worth a try.

We got an early start on our three-hour drive to Chicago. Mom wasn't all that fired up to go, but she agreed in time. I downed three antacid tablets before we left.

"I hope this place can help you get a job, a place of your own," I said to start the conversation.

"I'd rather be going to court to get you kids back."

She couldn't fend for herself. How could she take responsibility for us?

"Aunt Birdie told me you wouldn't get custody of us without having your own place."

"I don't give a rat's ass what Birdie says."

"Nice way to talk about the person who's giving you a place to stay."

I received a grunt in response.

"Chances are they're going to ask you what skills you have. Have you thought about that?"

"Who is?"

"The people at this place where we're going."

"I don't even know why we're going there. I'm not ready for it."

"When will you be ready for it?"

"Never. Maybe never."

So much for trying to help her. So much for gradually working my way up to a discussion about what happened four years earlier. So much for taking the high road.

"You want to tell me how Dad died?"

She didn't answer my question for several seconds. "Car accident."

"Were you in the car?"

"I was."

"So what happened?"

"He lost control of it and crashed into the back of a pickup truck."

"Were the streets wet, or was he going too fast, or what?"

"What happened to all our stuff at the house?" she asked.

"What stuff?"

"Any stuff."

"We took our clothes and as much other junk as we could fit in the suit-case before we left."

"Anything in the cellar?"

Interesting question.

"What? The emergency food and water or the Christmas decorations?"

"Don't be a smartass."

"There was nothing else in the cellar." Not a lie if she was talking about the main cellar, which of course I knew she wasn't.

"Why'd you leave anyway?" she asked.

"The house?"

"Yes, the house. Where else would I be talking about?"

"You received an eviction notice."

"We did?"

"Mm-hm."

"I didn't know that. But, no biggie. I knew you'd be safe with Birdie."

* * *

"How did it go?" I asked my mother as we walked to my car. While she had been talking with various people in the ex-offender reentry program, I sat in the waiting area reading year-old copies of *Newsweek, Sports Illustrated,* and *Good Housekeeping.*

"Waste of time."

"Based on their brochure—"

"Based on my first-hand experience, it was a waste of time. Let's go."

I have to admit that it had crossed my mind to ditch her—I could have easily outrun her.

"Okay, so you were in there two hours. Who did you talk with?"

"Two of your typical help-the-felon counselors."

"And what did they say?"

"What difference does it make?" she snapped.

"Because they are there to help you."

"If they really wanted to help me, they'd give me a supply of some decent bug juice."

"Bug juice?"

"Drugs…to make me feel less like shit."

"Are you going to tell me what they talked to you about?"

"Fine. One wanted to help me adjust to life on the outside, which I don't need. And they can keep the spiritual guidance crap. I don't need that either."

"They didn't talk about job training or placement, places to live, parenting classes, none of that?"

"The places I'd have to go to are too far away."

"From what?"

"You kids, of course."

"You can't even *see* Lucy without a court-approved supervisor."

"Where'd you hear that?"

"Aunt Birdie."

"That's bullshit. I'm going to court for custody. I'll show them."

"Go for it," I said, knowing she'd never get it without first jumping through all their hoops.

# Chapter 32

I became more uncomfortable with my mother each day, and to keep distance between us, I buried myself in sports and schoolwork, studying either in the school library or at Georgia's house. Thanks to Mom, I became quite a good student. It wasn't what she did or said so much that bothered me but rather what she didn't do or say. She lacked motivation to accomplish even the simplest of tasks, like make her bed in the morning or comb her hair, and her emotional flatness was enough to make me want to take her by the shoulders and shake her.

That left Aunt Birdie to deal with her, which I regretted, but since my aunt had made it clear that she was the decision-maker when it came to my mother's residency, I figured she'd brought that on herself.

I prayed that Mom would be gone by Thanksgiving, gone anywhere. But since that was only three weeks away, deep inside I knew that wasn't likely to happen. She had taken to sleeping until noon each day, then watching TV or playing solitaire in her room, coming out only when she smelled food. I asked Aunt Birdie how long she was going to put up with it.

"Ben, your mother has emphysema."

"How do you know that?"

"She told me."

"And you believe her?"

She gave me a look.

"Sorry, but I don't trust her."

"That chronic cough she has, the occasional hitch in her breathing—that's how I found out. I pushed her about it until she finally admitted that she had been diagnosed with it while she was in prison. Ever notice her feet and ankles?"

"No."

"She keeps them covered because they're swollen. Another symptom. I know. My husband died from emphysema."

"Your husband? I didn't know you were ever married."

"A hundred years ago."

"You're kidding."

"Long story…for another time."

"So that's why you're not kicking her out, because she has emphysema?"

"That and other things."

"All she's doing is using you. She's making no effort to get back on her feet. She—"

"I don't know that she has the wherewithal or the energy to get back on her feet."

"Aren't there medications she can take?"

"She has no money and no insurance."

"What do other people do?"

"I told her to apply for Medicaid, but she didn't seem receptive."

"That's plain stupid."

"Don't tell her I told you about what she's got. She asked me not to."

So it looked like Mom wasn't going anywhere and my aunt was okay with it. That sucked, and there wasn't a thing I could do about it.

* * *

Lucy and her foster family were going out of town for Thanksgiving. Georgia's mom invited the three of us over for the day—even after hearing the awful stories about my mother. But as much as I appreciated her kindness, I had to keep my mother from meeting Georgia's mother and her partner. The way my mother could run at the mouth without thinking and her crude language had all the earmarks of a disaster.

On Thanksgiving morning, I considered potential ways to keep my mother home for the day—none of which were remotely close to being honorable. I was reminded of Mrs. Franzen's lecture about taking the high road. Her words snapped me back to my senses.

But my fear of my mother ruining the holiday ended when she refused to leave the house.

"Why not join us, Rose?" Aunt Birdie said to her. "It will do you good to get out."

"No, thanks. I'd rather stay here."

"But you'll—"

"Would you lay off it, Birdie? I don't need to be around a couple of dykes all day. Had enough of that in prison."

My aunt looked disappointed in my mom's decision. I reveled in it.

Georgia greeted us at the door.

"Where's your mom?" Georgia's mother asked me after we'd settled in their living room.

"She wasn't feeling up to coming," I told her.

"That's too bad. I'll send you home with a plate of food for her."

After engaging in small talk with the adults, Georgia and I went downstairs to the family room, where we hung out until dinner.

"So what's the real reason you mother didn't come?" she asked me.

"I don't know. She's so screwed up. Lazy, no interest in anything, like she's lost or something."

"Maybe she is."

"My aunt thinks she's having a hard time with the transition from prison life. Like she got used to having all decisions made for her, and now she doesn't know how to act."

"Sad."

"Pathetic."

"What's going to happen to her?"

"I guess that's up to Aunt Birdie and how long she's willing to put up with her, which looks like it might be a long time."

"What was she like before all this happened? Was she a good mom?"

"I don't know. She worked six days a week, sometimes into the evening. We didn't see much of her."

"I can't imagine growing up without my mom around. I rely on her for everything."

"You got lucky."

"It must be rough not having a parent to go to, to ask their opinion on stuff, get their permission."

"You're forced to make tough choices, I'll tell you that."

"Ben?"

"Yeah."

"Do you love your mom?"

I didn't respond for the longest time.

"I don't know. It's hard to say I love her when I haven't forgiven her."

"So why don't you forgive her?"

"And let her off the hook…just like that? Nope."

"Why not?"

"Maybe if she'd own up to what she did. Maybe if she'd apologize for it and then ask for forgiveness…maybe then. I used to go to church with the Putnams. One of the sermons was all about forgiveness. And I distinctly remember the minister talking about how most of us need some kind of admission from the person who needs forgiving in order for us to actually forgive them. One of the few sermons I actually got something out of."

"And then did he go on to say, 'Do not judge, and you will not be judged. Do not condemn, and you will not be condemned. Forgive, and you will be forgiven.'? That's one of my mom's favorites."

"Actually, the minister was a woman."

"My bad."

"No, the verse I remembered was more like, if someone sins against you, let them have it, and if they say they're sorry, then you can forgive them. That's not exactly how it went, but it's close."

"Something may have been lost in the translation there."

"Maybe."

# Chapter 33

I entered the last semester of the school year feeling good after having maintained a C average. Given my lack of proper schooling for the first twelve years of my life, a part-time job, a busy basketball schedule, and Georgia, I was damn proud of myself. I shared my grades with my mother.

"Homeschooling was good enough before," she said.

"Not really. They placed me two grades behind kids my age when I enrolled in public school here."

"So that makes me a bad mother, I suppose."

"My point was just that—"

"Do you know how hard I had to work to provide for all of you? Putting up with that bitch day after day."

"Do you know how hard it was going to school for the first time in my life standing a head taller than kids two years younger than me?"

"If it wasn't for me, Ben, you'd be in foster care."

I glared at her in disbelief. "I *was* in foster care...*because* of you. Lucy *is* in foster care...*because* of you."

"Well, you would have been there a lot sooner if it hadn't been for my good parenting all those years."

"That's some logic you got there, Mom."

Aunt Birdie walked into the room.

"Everything okay in here?" she asked.

"Yes, warden," Mom said with sarcasm.

When she went into a long coughing jag, worse than usual, I wondered if it was a put-on to get sympathy.

"What can I get you, Rose?" Aunt Birdie asked. "Do you have an inhaler? Any medication left?"

She shook her head, rose from her chair, and walked toward her bedroom where she continued to cough.

"She should see a doctor if she's sick," I said.

"She won't go."

"Well, she should. Can't we force her?"

"I don't think so."

One more thing I didn't understand. You could force children who didn't know any better to do certain things, but not adults.

"And here's another thing I don't get. Lucy and I should be able to see each other whenever we want, not just on special occasions. She should be able to come here to visit by herself, and I should be able to go to the Larsens'. There's no good reason why—"

"Ben, everyone thinks the arrangement we have right now is working just fine. The social workers and others have been through this before. They know what's best."

"But I'm her brother, and no one discussed it with me."

"I know, and we all—"

"Who is *we all*?"

"CPS, her foster parents…and me too."

"This stinks. And here I thought you were on my side."

"I am on your side, sweetheart. And we want what's in her best interest, right?"

"I practically raised her."

"Ben, she went through a lot. The transition to foster care was rough for her. But now, now she's adjusting beautifully. Let's leave well enough alone."

"It's stupid."

"By the way, your caseworker is coming by tomorrow evening."

"I have basketball practice."

"You'll have to skip it."

"I can't skip it! Coach will—"

"You'll have to skip it."

I got up to go to my room. "Screw the rules," I mumbled on my way there.

"What did you say?"

"Nothing."

"Ben, come back here."

*Shit.*

"That's going to cost you three days without car privileges."

"What? You can't do that!"

"I can, and I will. I don't like your attitude lately."

"You're not my mother!"

"As your guardian, I have the same rights as a parent. And don't you forget it."

* * *

Aunt Birdie was using her "parental rights" to punish me. I hadn't seen that coming. I considered her more like…well, like an aunt. How were Georgia and I supposed to get to and from school? Basketball practice? My job at the grocery store? I confronted her the next day.

"Look, I'm sorry for mouthing off like I did. It won't happen again."

"The punishment stands."

"But Aunt Birdie, how am I supposed to get around?"

"You should have thought of that before."

"But I wasn't aware that you were going to do that. Shouldn't we have a list or something? You know, here's the crime, and here's the punishment. Like Mrs. Putnam had."

"Shall I see if Mrs. Putnam will take you back?"

I detected a smile lurking behind her stone face.

"Rule number 68. Do not leave any belongings lying around the house," I said, mimicking my former foster mom. "One item—no TV for a week. More than three items—no TV for a month. And if it's your underwear—no TV…ever."

She laughed. I knew she would.

"Rule number 983. No TV before nine o'clock in the morning, between eleven and two in the afternoon, after ten o'clock in the evening, on Sunday mornings, or when a yellow Volkswagen goes by."

"Stop making me laugh. I'm upset with you, remember?"

"I do, but I wish you weren't."

She stared at me, her lips pressed together in a thin line. "Okay. Now you know the consequences of bad behavior. Next time, I won't give in like this."

I hugged her and gave her a peck on her cheek. "I'm going over to Georgia's."

"What about basketball practice?"

"Doesn't start until six."

She gave me one of those aren't-you-forgetting-something looks.

"When will Mrs. Brownback be here?"

"Eight."

"I'll be home by then."

* * *

Georgia had a wide smile on her face when she opened the door to let me in.

I gave her a quick kiss, something I did now on a regular basis. As much as I wanted it to be more, I couldn't get up the nerve. I was comfortable talking with her, hanging out together, sharing my most personal thoughts, but when it came time to kiss her or even hold her hand, it suddenly became awkward for me. I was such a dork back then.

"You look like you just won the lottery. What gives?" I asked her.

"Let's go downstairs."

Once in their family room, she took my hands and said, "How'd you like to go to Cancun with us over Christmas?"

"What?"

"Mom said I could ask you. And guess what else."

"I have no idea."

"She and Zoe are going to get married there. Isn't that cool?"

"Married?"

"Well, not exactly. It's called a commitment ceremony. Same thing, but not legal."

"Wow. Yeah, that's awesome," I said, not knowing how I really felt about it.

"So you'll come?"

"I don't know. What are the dates?"

"We leave on the twenty-third and come back on January third. Mom said she'll cover your expenses."

"Wow."

"You said that already."

"Does that coincide with our school break?"

"Except for the twenty-third, but that's no biggie."

"I'd miss work and basketball."

She put both hands on her hips. "You mean you'd pick work and basketball over me?"

"It's not that. I'd want to make sure I had that job when I got back, and basketball, well, Coach Ryan is a stickler for attendance. And there's one more thing."

"You sure know how to break a girl's heart," she said with a turned-down lower lip.

"It's Aunt Birdie. She'd be there alone with Mom."

"So?"

"You know what she's like. Would you want to spend ten days alone with her?"

"You said your mom stays in her room all day."

"She does, but still…"

Georgia shrugged. "Well, if you don't want to go…"

I stood at the bottom of the stairs to block her from ascending them.

"I want to go. Just give me some time to work out a few things."

"You sure?"

"Ten days with you in Cancun? Are you kidding?"

Images of us walking along the beach together made my heart race.

# Chapter 34

Not being able to see Lucy whenever I wanted tore at me on a couple of different levels. It bothered me that I couldn't see for myself that she was consistently okay—even though in my head I knew she probably was. I was especially pissed that others had the power to forbid me to see her. The phone conversations and holiday visits we had helped, but more face-to-face interactions would have been far better.

Lucy was ten and in the fifth grade, the same grade they'd put me in when I was twelve. I wasn't allowed to go to her foster home to see her whenever I wanted, but no one had said anything about my visiting her at her school. And who would know if I did? I concocted a plan I was sure would work. But before I put it into gear, I asked Aunt Birdie about Cancun. She said she thought it would be a great experience.

"What about Mom?" I asked her.

"Don't worry about your mom. I'll handle it with her."

I asked her how she'd feel being alone with Mom for ten whole days, including Christmas.

"We'll be fine. You go and have a good time."

I called Georgia to let her know it was a go and to ask her if she would go shopping with me for appropriate clothes. We made plans for the following Saturday.

* * *

Lucy's school let out at 3:15, forcing me to ditch my last class in order to get to her school by then. I figured I could make up one English class with no problem.

After arriving at her school, I parked my car in a far corner of the lot, walked toward the side door, and waited behind a large tree. At 3:10, four busses pulled around to the door and waited. When the busses blocked my view of the door, I inched my way past the last one and situated myself closer to the building so I could see Lucy come out and what bus she got on.

The driver of Lucy's bus was busy talking to a student and didn't see me step in. When Lucy spotted me, she gasped. I signaled her to shush and sat down beside her.

"What are you doing here, Benny?"

"I came to see you. I miss you, little buddy."

"Vet told me you could only come see me on special occasions."

"I know, and that sucks, but this is okay."

"Are you coming home with me?"

"Just to your bus stop, then I'll get off."

"Then where will you go?"

"I'll walk back to my car at your school. It's not that far."

"I'm glad you came, Benny."

"How are you doing? Still like it with the Larsens?"

"Yep. How's Mom?"

No one had ever told Lucy about Mom being in prison. As far as she knew, she had been away for a long time dealing with several medical problems and was now living with us.

"No complaints?" I asked her.

"Nope."

"Everyone treats you okay?"

"Yep. How's Mom?"

"She's okay. She still needs help though."

"What kind of help?"

"I don't know. Help to find a job, a different place to live. She's kind of lost, if you ask me."

"What's she like?"

"She's okay."

"Is she nice?"

"Sometimes."

A look of sadness crept across her face. "I don't remember her, Benny. Can I see her?"

"In time. Then you'll get to know her again. Like I have."

"I'm almost home. When will I see you again?"

"Soon, I hope. In the meantime, no one said we had to stop talking on the phone."

"This is my stop. Are you getting off too?"

"Yep."

Mrs. Larsen was at the bus stop waiting for Lucy and the twins. I stayed in my seat until the four of them had turned and were walking toward their car. But as soon as I stepped off the bus, I knew I was in trouble—Aunt Birdie and Mrs. Brownback stood within a few feet of me with their arms crossed.

*Shit.*

"I'm busted, aren't I?" I said with a sheepish grin.

Aunt Birdie grabbed my arm without saying anything and led me to Mrs. Brownback's car, making me think I was in more trouble than originally anticipated.

"You were aware of the visitation decision and went to see Lucy anyway."

"She's my sister."

"But you were told visits would be limited for a while."

"I didn't go to her house."

"And your point is?"

"I thought it would be okay on school grounds."

"Really?"

I nodded. "I had to make sure she was okay. See for myself. I didn't think it was a big deal."

"Well, you were wrong. Ditching school, defying our decision is a big deal."

"No one is going to tell me I can't see my sister."

"You don't get it, do you?"

Not understanding the relevancy of her question, I dug in my heels.

"No, *you* don't get it," I said, not realizing even right afterward that this was the worst thing I could have said.

When we reached my car in Lucy's school parking lot, Aunt Birdie said, "I'm so disappointed in you, Benjamin. This was a stupid stunt you pulled today, and you're going to pay for it."

On our way home, I asked my aunt how she knew about what I had done.

"Apparently one of the kids on the bus told the driver that a high school kid was on the bus talking to Lucy. The bus driver called the school. The school called her social worker, and it was her social worker who called me."

"Geez, can't get away with anything."

"I hope you realize the seriousness of this, Ben."

"Sure." I didn't really.

"I'm not sure you do." Aunt Birdie was pretty astute. "There will be consequences for your actions."

"What kind of consequences?"

"That trip to Cancun?"

"What about it?"

"You're not going."

"What?"

"You're not going."

"You can't do that!"

"Yes, I can."

"Get real. There was no harm done, and I get to visit her anyway on other occasions."

"You defied our rules, Ben. You can't do that. And on top of that, you ditched a class to do it."

"What I did was nothing! Why are you being so mean? Give me some small punishment, but don't take away my trip."

"The fact that you think it was a small thing worries me even more. Mrs. Brownback and I discussed what the consequences for your actions should be, and we think disallowing you to go on the trip is appropriate."

"That trip has nothing to do with what I did. This is so bogus."

"It has everything to do with it. You used incredibly poor judgment today. You think I feel comfortable allowing you to go off to another country with your girlfriend where you'll be faced with judgment calls left and right? No, I don't."

"Her mom will be there—it's not like we're going alone."

"Her mom will be a little preoccupied, don't you think?"

"So what? There will still be two adults around."

"You need to fully understand right versus wrong and the consequences for choosing wrong before being trusted with anything big, like going to

Mexico with your girlfriend's family. Better to understand that now rather than later in life…like your mother."

"So much for family. I guess it would have been better if I didn't give a shit about Lucy."

"Keep it up, Ben. There are other privileges I can take away."

Despite the freezing temperature, a hot flush ran through my body. At the time, I thought she was being incredibly unfair. What was I supposed to tell Georgia?

The idea of spending winter break with my mother and aunt while Georgia was in Cancun made me think about running away.

* * *

Home life during the next several days sucked—my attitude fluctuated daily depending on which emotion had risen to the surface. I hated everyone, including myself, but most of all my mother. I wouldn't have been in the position I was in if it hadn't been for her. I avoided her, knowing that if I spent any amount of time with her, I would end up telling her off. And Aunt Birdie wasn't on my list of champions either.

My worst moment was when I called Georgia to tell her I couldn't go to Cancun. I had waited a few days, hoping Aunt Birdie would have a change of heart, but she didn't.

"Why did you do a stupid thing like that?" Georgia asked.

That wasn't the response I had expected.

"You don't get it."

"Oh, I get it alright. You were told to stay away from Lucy, and you did it anyway. Not very smart."

"You don't have brothers or sisters, so you don't understand."

"I don't need brothers or sisters to know not to do that."

"I wish—"

"No problem. I'll find someone else to go. Bye."

Five minutes later, my phone rang.

"I'm sorry I said that," Georgia said. "I was so looking forward to our trip and disappointed when you said you weren't coming. I shouldn't have said what I did."

I told her not to worry about it, even though it did bother me. The week preceding her trip to Cancun, we talked only a few times. Things between us had changed, and that caused painful emotions. My juvenile, immature mind blamed everyone but myself.

Wasting away the first morning of my Christmas break in bed, my mind drifted back five years to when fate had brought Lucy and me together with Melvin. One of the most vivid memories I had was him telling me to always do the right thing. Pretty ironic advice coming from someone who had spent time in jail on more than one occasion, drank in between AA meetings, stole an item from my suitcase, and technically kidnapped us.

Still, I never forgot his advice. When the light bulb finally went on and I realized I was contributing to the crummy atmosphere in our household, I knew I needed to be the one to change it. Lord knew my mother wasn't going to change.

Of course, realizing that was one thing. Doing something about it was something else.

# Chapter 35

"You're spending Christmas Day with Lucy, right?" Aunt Birdie asked me two days prior to the holiday.

"Yes, and you?"

"I don't think that would be fair to your mother."

My mother had not made any attempt to arrange for supervised visits with Lucy. But as I later learned from my aunt—for reasons I didn't understand at the time and still don't—she could have. As much as this bothered me, and as difficult as it was for me to hold back, I didn't say anything. Instead, I tried to make things better between us.

"Can we plan it so I'm here for part of the day and with the Larsens the other part?"

"Is that what you want?"

"Yeah."

She smiled a smile that said, *I hear you, but I don't believe you.*

"And Aunt Birdie?"

"Yes."

"I put aside some money from work, enough for me to pick up something for dinner on Christmas Eve. Would that be okay?"

"Come here."

When I reached her, she gave me a hug and said into my shirt, "It's good to have you back, sweetie."

"What's this all about?" my mother asked when she entered the room and observed us in a hug. "A lovefest?"

We parted, and Aunt Birdie said, "Yes, it is. Want to make something of it?"

After an uncomfortable pause, we all laughed.

"We were just making plans for Christmas. Ben is going to treat us to dinner on Christmas Eve, and I was thinking of making a big, old traditional dinner on Christmas Day. I haven't done that in years. But I'll need your help…both of you."

"I'm in," I said.

"Looks like I have no choice," said my mother.

"Sure, you do," said Aunt Birdie. "You can sit and mope in your bedroom all day until dinner is ready, then come out to eat and go back in there as soon as you're through, or you can be part of this family, make yourself useful, and contribute to the festivities. It's your choice, Rose."

*You go, Aunt Birdie.*

I wished I had realized it then—that Aunt Birdie's standing up to my mother was her way of letting me know that she respected me and that she understood how I felt about my mother's lackadaisical demeanor. It gave me a good feeling, though years later.

* * *

Before I ordered Chinese food for our Christmas Eve meal, I knocked on my mother's bedroom door to ask her what she preferred. When she didn't answer, I opened it a crack and found her slumped over in a chair, her body visibly trembling.

"Mom?"

When she didn't respond, I approached her and called to her again.

"Aunt Birdie!" I shouted.

Aunt Birdie rushed into the room.

"Call 9-1-1!" she said. "She's having a seizure."

I ran for my phone, dialed the number, and described my mother's condition to the operator.

After taking down our address, she asked several more questions.

"Is she breathing? Is she on any medication? Has she had seizures before?"

I didn't know the answer to any of them.

"Aunt Birdie, is she breathing?" I yelled from the other room.

"Yes," she shouted back.

I ran back into my mom's bedroom—where my aunt was trying to keep her vertical in the chair—and told the operator I didn't see any pill bottles. She advised us to allow my mother to complete the seizure and not restrain her. The ambulance was on its way.

Aunt Birdie kneeled next to my mom and held her hand while I stood there paralyzed, my heart racing.

"Go outside to flag down the ambulance," my aunt told me. She was much better at handling emergencies than I was.

I did as told, and by the time the paramedics arrived, my mom had stopped shaking and appeared to be asleep.

"That sometimes happens," said one of the paramedics.

Aunt Birdie told them about my mom's emphysema.

"You don't know if she's on any medications for it?"

"She might have some, but I don't know what or where they are."

"Some medications for COPD can cause seizures, but they're generally not used anymore," one paramedic said as they lifted Mom onto the gurney.

"Where are you taking her?" I asked.

"Midwest Medical Center in Galena. Do you know where that is?"

I told him I did.

After the paramedics left, we searched Mom's room and unearthed about fifteen pill bottles—some of them empty, some containing a few pills—none of which were familiar to Aunt Birdie. We placed all of them in a bag and took them with us to the hospital. Mom was in the ER when we arrived. As soon as we connected with a nurse, we gave her the bag containing Mom's cache of drugs.

Waiting was the worst part—the uncertainty of what they were doing to her, hoping she wasn't suffering too much. Nothing else mattered to me— not even missing my trip to Cancun. While Aunt Birdie droned on about relatively unimportant stuff—bingo, the weather, what Christmas cookies we were going to make—I spent the entire time watching the wall clock and the door, desperate for news from someone who knew what was going on with Mom. My aunt's chatter was a helpful distraction.

When the doctor finally came in, I studied his face for an indication of good news or bad.

"She's okay," he said before sitting down. "We have her in the ICU. Your mother suffers from emphysema—I don't know if you knew that."

"Yes, we know."

"And high blood pressure…and hepatitis C."

I looked at Aunt Birdie, who seemed as surprised as I was.

"I talked to her about the medications that had been prescribed to her when she was in prison. Some of them I question, but that may be neither here nor there since she admitted to me she doesn't take them regularly."

"Can you prescribe new ones?" Aunt Birdie asked.

"I can, and I will. The drug she took right before she had the seizure is known for causing seizures. We stopped prescribing it years ago—there are better ones available now."

"Can we see her?" I asked.

"Sure. Come with me."

Mom didn't look well—pale, haggard, lifeless. Sad.

"How are you feeling?" I asked her.

"Like shit. How do you think I feel?"

Typical response for my mother.

"The doctor said you're going to be alright. Did he tell you how long you have to be here?"

"Overnight, at least. I don't know after that."

"Well, we'll save Christmas dinner for you," my aunt told her. "You just take your time getting better."

"I'll do that."

* * *

"Can I ask you something, Ben?" Aunt Birdie said on the drive home from the hospital.

"Sure."

"What was your mom like growing up?"

I laughed. "That seems like a hundred years ago."

"I was just curious."

"To be honest, we didn't see too much of her. When we got up in the morning, she had already gone to work, and we usually got hungry before she got home at night, so we didn't eat dinner with her."

"What about your dad?"

"You know he drank."

"Yes, I know."

"Well, he drank a lot."

"How about on weekends? Did you do things as a family then?"

"Not very often. Mom worked on Saturdays. On Sundays, she was busy doing housework, going to the grocery store, laundry—all the stuff she couldn't do during the week, I guess."

"And your dad?"

"He didn't do much around the house."

"I wish he'd gotten help with his drinking years ago, right after…"

"After what?"

"Nothing."

"Aunt Birdie?"

"What?"

"Is she going to be okay?"

"I hope so, Ben. I hope so."

# Chapter 36

Aunt Birdie and I went through the motions of enjoying Christmas, but with Mom in the hospital, it wasn't easy. We worried about her physical health but thought something had to be wrong with her mentally as well. She had no ambition or motivation to get back on her feet to prepare for the day that she'd be eligible to take custody of us. I asked my aunt about it after my visit with Lucy.

"Maybe she sees how well you're doing here, and Lucy in her foster home, and thinks she's not needed anymore," she said.

"I never thought of it like that."

"And she doesn't know how to turn that around."

"She refuses to get help."

"I know. Maybe when she gets home, we can change that."

Aunt Birdie had a whole different take on Mom than I did. I hated her bad behavior. Aunt Birdie tried to understand it. She wasn't even related to her, yet she was the one who was reaching out. That was eye-opening for me, more so when I got older.

"How was your visit with Lucy?" she asked.

"Good."

"That's all? Just good?"

I laughed. "I'm still kind of bummed that she's doing so well."

"Why?"

"Because I wanted to do that for her."

* * *

I picked Mom up from the hospital the day after Christmas.

"Come in, dear," Aunt Birdie said to her when she arrived. "Welcome home. We're so glad you're okay. Come in the living room where I've got a fire going."

"I'm tired. I think I'll lie down for a while," my mother said.

"I've planned a whole Christmas dinner for us. Will you let me know when you're hungry?"

"Mm-hm."

I would have told her what time we were eating and left it at that.

I told Aunt Birdie that I had the opportunity to work full-time the following week during my school break. I asked her if that would be a problem.

"Of course not."

"What about Mom?"

"She'll be fine. Her doctor gave me her medicine schedule, and I'll make sure she takes it on time. He said that should help with her energy, swollen ankles and feet, and even her weight."

"It wasn't her I was worried about," I told her.

"I'm a big girl. I can handle your mom."

* * *

Georgia preoccupied my thoughts while she was in Cancun, and I wondered if maybe she did bring someone else with her. I figured I'd find out when I picked her up for school on Monday.

In the meantime, I saw little of my mother the week following Christmas—I was busy working during the day and at basketball practice many evenings. The few times we did talk, she seemed out of it. I asked my aunt about it.

"One of the medications makes her woozy, I think—the one she takes after dinner. It says on the bottle that she shouldn't drive after taking it. I can see why."

"I notice she's not coughing as much," I said. "Thanks for paying for these new meds, Aunt Birdie. I know you didn't have to do that. Any talk about what she's going to do with the rest of her life?"

"We've discussed it."

"No progress, right?"

"Not too much."

I wasn't hopeful.

* * *

On the day before the first day back to school, I called Georgia to ask her about her trip and tell her that I'd pick her up at the regular time on Monday.

"Um…I'll catch you at school, Ben. See you then."

It was over. I had desperately hung on to the hope of things getting back to normal when she returned. It was incredible how one conversation could change your whole life.

It was all my fault. Still, I thought she could have been a little more understanding of my situation. Thoughts of the fun times we'd had together spun in my head—the long talks over movies we'd seen, holding hands, the kisses. No words could describe the way it felt to fall from the high I had been on when we'd been together.

I dreaded seeing her in school. She was a grade behind me, but we passed each other in the halls between classes all the time, and we had the same lunch period. I dreaded it so much that I made it a point to look at the walls when I passed through the halls of the school that first day, and instead of going into the lunchroom at noon, I sat in my car for a half hour so I wouldn't run into her. I never should have turned on the radio—"Without You" was our song.

During sixth-period gym, I found out that I'd made the varsity basketball team, allowing me to temporarily forget about my break-up with Georgia and feel on top of the world for the rest of the afternoon. First sophomore to have ever made the team. Coach called me "Big Ben." I liked that.

Deciding I couldn't go through another school day avoiding Georgia, I called her that evening. After we got through exchanging the requisite pleasantries, I asked her what happened to us.

"It just didn't work out, Ben. That happens, you know."

"I know."

"We're very different."

"Oh, I know."

"So we need to move on."

"We can still be friends," I said.

"Oh, sure," she said, but I knew it wouldn't be the same.

When I came out of my room, Aunt Birdie asked me how my day went.

"Crappy."

"What? But you love school."

"I didn't love it today."

"Want to talk about it?"

I shrugged.

"Does it have anything to do with Georgia?"

I shrugged again.

"I can be a good listener, you know."

"She dumped me."

"I figured that."

"You never said anything."

"You needed your space," she said.

"Thanks for that."

"I know what it's like to lose someone you want to be with. But you know something? It gets better. I promise you that."

"I hope so, 'cause I don't think I could feel any worse."

I had been feeling so sorry for myself that I'd almost forgotten about the good news of the day.

"Guess what!"

"What?"

"I made the varsity basketball team."

"Really?"

"First sophomore to ever make the team."

"You're kidding."

"Well, it helped that two players got injured and are out for the rest of the season, and the coach was probably desperate."

"That doesn't change a thing—you made it!"

"What's all the commotion out here?" Mom entered the room in her bathrobe.

"Your son made the varsity basketball team!"

"That's nice."

I studied her face—her eyes darted from one side of me to the other.

"Are you alright?" I asked.

She attempted to take a step forward and came close to losing her balance.

Aunt Birdie jumped up and guided her back to her room. When my aunt came back a few minutes later, she had a worried look on her face.

"Is it the meds?" I asked.

"I think so, although it hasn't been this bad until now."

Mom didn't join us for dinner. I went to her room afterward to check on her.

"Are you okay, Mom?"

She motioned for me to come nearer. As I approached her, her eyes glided closed.

"It was an accident," she whispered, the thin thread of her voice echoing throughout the room.

# Chapter 37

When my mother whispered to me "It was an accident," I thought maybe she had wet herself. Not knowing how to deal with that, I summoned my aunt and told her. She checked to see if that had happened as she helped Mom into bed.

"What made you think that, Ben? She seemed fine to me," Aunt Birdie asked me when we returned to the living room.

"She mumbled something about having an accident," I told her. "Maybe I misunderstood her."

But I knew I hadn't misunderstood what she'd said, and I hadn't misunderstood the pain on her face when she'd said it.

The next opportunity I had to talk to my mother came a few days later, after dinner.

"Mom, don't go back to your room yet, okay?"

"I'm tired."

I didn't know how she could be tired—she'd slept most of the day.

"Let's talk."

She sat back down, with reluctance.

"How are you feeling with your new medicine and everything?"

"Fine."

"Just fine?"

"The other stuff didn't make me so sleepy."

"Did you make a doctor's appointment, like you were told to do?"

"No."

"Want me to make the appointment for you?"

"No."

"The hospital doctor thought that you should—"

"I really don't care what he thinks I should or shouldn't do."

"Do you care about anything, Mom?"

She got up and left the room. Aunt Birdie and I exchanged glances and shook our heads. I followed Mom to her room.

"Can I come in?" I asked her.

"Fine."

"The other night I came into your room and you said something about having an accident."

"I didn't have an accident."

"You were drowsy and fell asleep right afterward, so maybe you had just taken one of your meds."

"I didn't have an accident."

"Could you have been talking about Dad's accident?"

"That was probably it. I'm tired now."

I wasn't sure why her initial comment about the accident haunted me so, but it did.

* * *

The rest of my sophomore year flew by—homework, varsity basketball, working part-time, taking Aunt Birdie on errands. Lucy was doing so well that I now had unlimited visits with her, which also took up time. But no one heard me complain as it helped to take my mind off Georgia, who had moved on to another boyfriend—captain of the debate team.

Lucy was growing into a great kid. Gone was the shy little girl who had agreed with most anything anyone told her. She now had opinions of her own and expressed them effortlessly. Even though I was sad that I'd had nothing to do with her maturing, still I was happy for her.

My basketball coach, who had also become my mentor, encouraged me to think about college. When I told him there was no way I could afford to go to college, he gave me several brochures on schools offering basketball scholarships. He believed I was that talented. He told me if I kept up my game and GPA, my chances were good.

The thought of going to college both scared and excited me. I talked it over with Aunt Birdie one evening.

"You should go for it, Ben. You can do it."

Mom appeared in the doorway, in her nightgown, her hair tousled like she had just gotten out of bed. "He can do what?"

"My coach thinks I should apply for a basketball scholarship."

"Whusat?"

I glanced at Aunt Birdie, who looked as puzzled by her demeanor as I was. "Schmolarship?"

Mom appeared to be drunk. My aunt rose up from her chair, took Mom by the arm, and led her back to her bedroom.

"Is she okay?" I asked when she returned.

"I don't know. I've never seen her like this. She's asleep now."

"Is she drunk?"

"I don't know how—there's no alcohol in the house. Must be the meds."

After Aunt Birdie retired for the day, I went to check on Mom. I found her in her room slumped in a chair, drool sliding down her chin. When I touched her arm, she jumped.

"I didn't do it!" she shouted.

"What didn't you do?"

She stared at me with such fear in her eyes that it caused me to take a step back.

"You woke me up. Why'd you do that?"

"I'm sorry. I was just checking on you," I said taking a few more steps backward.

"Stay. I want you to stay."

She slurred her words, but I could still understand her. I sat down on the edge of her bed.

"Are you okay?" I asked.

"No, I'm not okay. I'll never be okay."

"Sure, you will. The doctor in the hospital said—"

"He don't know shit."

"Yes, he does. You just—"

"It was an accident, you know."

"What was an accident?"

"That day."

"What day?"

"That day."

She closed her eyes.

"Mom?"

She mumbled something I didn't understand.

"Mom?"

She didn't respond. She appeared to be asleep.

* * *

Mom had her good days and her bad days that summer. Even though Aunt Birdie was able to get her in to see a doctor once, she didn't want to go back to him, and her non-refillable prescriptions were running low.

"Let's take her in to see the doctor whether she likes it or not," I told my aunt.

"I'll hold her down while you drive?" she said through a smile.

"Something like that."

"I think we need a better plan."

I agreed but didn't have another one to offer.

One night toward the end of the summer, I was passing by my mother's door on the way to my room when I noticed the light on. It was around midnight, well past her usual bedtime. I peeked in and found her staring out the window, her back to me.

"Can't sleep?" I asked her.

She turned around, her eyes red and watery.

"What's wrong?" I asked.

She shook her head.

"Well, something's wrong. You've been crying."

She turned around to face the window.

"It's the medicine," she whispered.

"The medicine is making you cry?"

"The medicine is making me think about things."

"Sad things?"

"Terrible things."

"What terrible things?"

"You don't want to know."

"Sure, I do."

"No, you don't. I'm tired now."

"You want me to leave?"

"Yes."

Her words scared me, but not as much as her eerily calm disposition. That wasn't Mom.

* * *

First day of my junior year, I was pumped. Not only was I on the varsity basketball team, I was the starting center—a prestigious position I figured would raise my status among my peers, especially with girls. But juggling my course load of Algebra II, World History, Introduction to Computers, and Molecular Biology along with everything else wouldn't be easy. I considered quitting my part-time job at the grocery store, but without that, I wouldn't have money for gas, and I didn't want to have to ask Aunt Birdie for money.

My aunt finally goaded Mom into going back to her doctor. This time, Aunt Birdie went in with her and told the doctor about the effect the pills had on her. He still believed it was the right combination and wrote prescriptions for refills, something that surprised both Aunt Birdie and me.

After an especially late basketball practice one evening, I came home dead tired and went straight to bed. I closed my eyes, thinking of the awesome shots I had made. Before sleep took over, a loud thump came from somewhere in the house. I couldn't tell from where it came. When it occurred a second time, I got up to investigate.

The spray of light coming from under Mom's door told me she was still awake or had fallen asleep with the light on again. I peeked in to find her kneeling on her bed, holding a pillow high above her head.

"Hey, what are you doing?" I asked.

She glared at me with wild eyes, as if I had caught her about to do something inappropriate. She put the pillow down, rolled herself up into a ball, buried her face in her hands, and began to rock back and forth.

I walked toward her. "Mom? What's wrong?"

"I can't talk about it," she wailed.

"What can't you talk about?"

She continued rocking but said no more.

"Mom, talk to me. You can't keep doing this."

"No," she said.

"I'm not leaving until you tell me what's going on with you."

"She died because of me."

# Chapter 38

"What are you talking about?" I was afraid the meds were altering her speech, her thoughts.

"It was an accident," she said, her face still buried in her hands.

"Mom, I can't understand you when you talk into your hands."

She looked up and stared at me with vacant eyes. "I think these meds are wrong for me."

"Tell me about this accident."

"Mrs. Washington."

A punch to my gut would have had less impact on me. I sat down and took in several long, deep breaths.

"What happened with Mrs. Washington?" I asked, barely getting the words out.

"She shouldn't have gotten in my face like that," she said, focusing her gaze past me at something presumably on the wall. "And if she didn't have so much goddamn artfax in her house, it wouldn't have happened."

"Mom, can you start at the beginning? What happened that day?"

She leaned her back and head against the wall, her legs straight out in front of her on the bed, reminding me of one of Lucy's long-legged dolls.

"It took the old bat long enough to catch on to my taking her things."

"What kinds of things?"

She shrugged. "Knickknacks. The kind that are worth a lot of money. She had a ton of them and didn't notice anything missing for months…until that day." She paused as if to recall specific details. "This stupid little Hello Kitty thing—that's what she noticed missing from the curio cabinet in her bedroom."

I sat on my ice-cold hands, hoping the weight of my body would make their numbness go away.

"Why?" I asked her.

"Why what?"

"Why did you take things from her?"

"We couldn't live on the measly salary she paid me, and I didn't think she'd miss them, she had so much of the stuff."

"What did you do with the things you took, sell them?" I asked as if I didn't know.

"I just held on to them, until the money ran out."

"What money?"

"I took money from her all the time."

"You took money from her?"

"She always had money lying around. If she left two hundred on the bureau, I'd take fifty. She never knew how much was there. She liked paying people in cash—all us servants—to avoid taxes probably."

"So what did she say to you when she discovered the Hello Kitty thing missing?"

"She asked me if I'd seen it. I said 'no,' of course. Then she checked on her other collections, and the more she looked at them, the angrier she got. But then she disappeared into her bedroom for the longest time, so I assumed the whole thing was going to blow over."

"But it didn't."

"No, it didn't. She came back and shoved a long list in my face and asked me if I knew anything about the items, and when I said I didn't, she called me a goddamned liar."

Dumbfounded, I sat there shaking my head while she told the story.

"I told her it could have been any number of people who took her stuff—cleaning ladies, the cook, the gardener, the dry cleaner who brought her clothes into her bedroom and hung them up for her whenever he came. There were a lot of delivery people. I told her she was too trusting."

"Looks like she was."

"Then she got right in my face and accused me of stealing from her…so I pushed her."

"You pushed her…how hard?"

"Not that hard…but hard enough, I guess, for her to fall backward. Her cane went flying and she crashed into this pedestal thing with a bust of

George Washington on it, bronze or something. It was heavy, anyway." She paused, sniffled, and looked past me. "And it fell on her head."

"Oh, shit—"

"When something that heavy falls on your head from four feet up, well, I don't think she knew what hit her."

"So…she was dead?"

"I didn't know. I was too afraid to touch her."

"What did you do?"

"I called your father."

"Why didn't you call 9-1-1?"

"I didn't want to get blamed for it."

"But—"

"Hey, you put yourself in that position and see what *you* would do."

"So you called Dad."

"And he came. He wasn't afraid to touch her, and after he did, he told me she wasn't breathing, had no pulse or nothing. Then he freaked out and poured himself a stiff drink."

"That's Dad," I mumbled.

"Don't you talk about the dead like that, young man."

"Sorry."

"We filled a trash bag with a bunch of her other things and hightailed it out of there."

"You stole more stuff and then just left her there?"

"What could we do? She was dead."

"Right."

"Anyway, your dad was driving way too fast, and I kept telling him to slow down, but he'd had a couple of drinks at her house, and he was still wigged out about the whole thing." She teared up. "I kept telling him to slow down. He kept telling me to shut up. When he went too fast around the curve, he drove right into the back of a truck that had stopped for a stop sign. I walked away from it. He didn't. The ambulance came. I rode to the hospital with him in the back, unconscious, nearly dead, I guess. That's when I called you guys to let you know what happened."

"You never called us."

"I tried, but it said our number was disconnected. I was so nervous I thought I must have dialed wrong, so I called again. When I got the same recording, I figured they must have cut our service again. We were a little behind with some of the bills."

"Yeah, like the rent."

She stared at me until I had to look away.

"Like the rent," she repeated. "I'm really tired. I'm going to go to bed now."

"Will you tell me the rest tomorrow?"

"We'll see."

* * *

I lay in bed with my eyes wide open, knowing there was no way I was going to get any sleep that night, what was left of it. But I had school the next day, or did I? She had me so discombobulated, I didn't even know the day of the week. I turned on the TV to a news station. It was two a.m., Saturday, September 10. Oh, my God. September 10—five years to the day since Lucy and I left our home in the Ford Bronco. How ironic was that?

I mulled over in my head everything she'd said, trying to remember all the sordid details. After the third or fourth run-through, it hit me—another person had been charged with Mrs. Washington's death, the gardener. I grabbed the laptop I'd received for my birthday from Aunt Birdie and searched for articles on Mrs. Washington's death.

According to a newspaper article I found, thirty-eight-year-old Ricardo Reyes was initially charged with second-degree murder and grand theft but pleaded "not guilty" to both charges. He claimed to have been power-washing Mrs. Washington's patio when through the patio doors he spotted her foot. He let himself in to see if she was alright, and when he couldn't find her pulse, he called 9-1-1. He was later convicted of involuntary manslaughter and sentenced to seven years in prison. He had two years to go. The article didn't elaborate as to what evidence they had based his conviction on but went on to say that the grand-theft charges against him had been dropped.

Ricardo Reyes was serving a prison sentence for something my mother had done.

# Chapter 39

While Aunt Birdie and Leah were out shopping the next morning, I staked out Mom's bedroom door from the living room. She didn't come out until noon, and when she did, she grabbed a yogurt from the fridge and went right back in. I followed her and rapped on her door. When I received no response, I opened it.

"Can I come in?" I asked.

"Looks like you already have."

"I'd like to hear the rest of the story."

"I'm done talking."

"Mom, you can't give me half of it and then stop."

"I shouldn't have given you any of it. Damn meds screwed with my head."

"Don't you think—"

"I'd like to be alone now."

Knowing it would be a losing battle to keep arguing with her, I closed her door and returned to the living room. Finding nothing interesting on TV, I grabbed my laptop and searched the Internet for more articles on the incident. I had to know everything that went on that day. Here I was holding on to a box full of valuable items that had been stolen and possible knowledge of an innocent man in prison and a guilty woman not.

After an hour of searching and finding nothing new, it occurred to me that maybe court transcripts were available from my mom's and Reyes's trials. I Googled "how to find trial transcripts" and learned that court records were generally open to the public from the County Clerk's office. Their website didn't indicate whether their records were available online, so I called them and was told I could look up the case numbers by going to a different website, keying in the county, and following the prompts from there. Once I had the case numbers, the County Clerk could provide me with the court reporter's contact information so I could request the transcripts. I followed the instructions.

In the meantime, I continued to try to convince Mom to tell me more of the story, but to no avail. She had shut down.

*　*　*

Ten days after my mother's confession about Mrs. Washington's horrendous demise, I had transcripts from both trials. Reading them took days and proved to be quite the learning experience. The transcript for my mother's case was 157 pages long, most of which I skimmed. Three things stood out for me.

My mother never testified on her own behalf, but the public defender representing her said it had been my father who had stolen the items from Mrs. Washington's home and my mother hadn't even been aware of it. That wasn't what Mom had told me. The judge must have found that hard to believe as well, since he had found her guilty.

The second thing I found interesting was that her lawyer had claimed that Mrs. Washington had been alive and well when my mother left her home that day. My mother had claimed that she wasn't feeling well while working in the Washington home and had called her husband to pick her up. That was also a lie.

And the last thing I learned was the amount of time Mom's lawyer had talked about her undying devotion to her children, how she had homeschooled her son his entire life and had just started doing the same for her daughter. Really? We had been lucky if she remembered to give us an assignment before she left for work each day.

The transcript for Ricardo Reyes proved more enlightening…and disturbing. He did testify on his own behalf and claimed he had found Mrs. Washington dead and immediately called 9-1-1, which he believed was the right thing to do. He testified that he had never hurt another human being or stolen anything in his entire life and said he couldn't live with himself or God if he had. But the prosecutor made a good case against him with circumstantial evidence. What I found particularly disturbing was that the prosecutor kept asking Reyes to repeat his answers, saying he didn't understand what he was saying, and some of the prosecutor's questions were confusing even to me. Reyes kept apologizing, saying his English wasn't so good.

After deliberating for six hours, the jury had come back with a verdict of guilty on the involuntary manslaughter charge.

I was convinced Ricardo Reyes was an innocent man.

* * *

As hard as I tried to catch Mom at a time when she was a little crazed on her meds so she'd volunteer more information as to what happened at the Washington residence, I couldn't time it right given my busy schedule and her constant seclusion. The few times I had the chance, Aunt Birdie was there. I didn't see the need to involve her at this point, especially since everything Mom had told me so far had been said while she was under the influence of drugs.

A week later, the opportunity presented itself when Aunt Birdie was at church.

Mom stumbled out of her room almost crashing into a floor lamp. I jumped up from the living room sofa to help stabilize her and got her to sit down.

"Goddamn drugs. At least with alcohol, you get to enjoy the ride."

"Aren't you about due for another doctor visit?" Aunt Birdie had taken her the last time and, I suspected, had paid for it. "Maybe he can give you something else."

"He already said he couldn't. I wanted to just stop taking them, but nothing gets past Nurse Ratched here."

My ears perked up at that reference. Evidence that she knew Melvin and/ or his sister? Or merely a coincidence?

"You said you'd tell me what happened after the car accident."

"I did?"

"Mm-hm. You said you were at the hospital with Dad and you tried to call us, but the phone had been disconnected."

"Oh, yeah. I called Birdie, who said she'd come get you. Which she did."

"Not exactly."

"You're here, aren't you?"

"Yeah, but she didn't come get us. By the time we made our way here, she was in the hospital."

"Made your way here?"

"I'll tell about that some other time."

She slumped over in the chair. I hoped I wasn't going to lose her.

"So you're at the hospital with Dad."

"He was in bad shape—I didn't want to leave him. And you guys were… or so I thought. Anyway, smashed-up car was towed. Cops found the bag full of stuff. Stupid…"

"Did Dad die in the hospital?"

"Yeah, alone. Damn cops dragged my ass off to the station."

"They came to the hospital first?"

"Asked me a bunch of stupid questions. I screwed up the answers. The next thing I knew, two Barneys escorted me to their squad car in handcuffs. Bastards. They knew he was dying."

"So then what?"

"I got arrested for grand theft. And that one phone call I made? It was to Birdie, letting her know where I was."

I tried to pin the pieces of her story to the timeline as I remembered it, and it didn't make sense that she'd talked to Birdie the same day all this went down.

"You actually talked to her?"

"I don't know. Maybe I left a message."

That made more sense.

"Did you know we ended up in different foster homes?"

"Later." She hung her head down. "I knew it later," she mumbled. She rose from the sofa and sauntered back to her bedroom. I followed her.

"You have to turn yourself in, Mom."

"Are you shittin' me? I did my time."

"That gardener is in jail for something you did!"

"A jury found him guilty, so be it."

"You said yourself that Mrs. Washington had no pulse when you left."

"No, I didn't."

"Yes, you did."

"No, I must have said she didn't have much of a pulse."

"No, you didn't. I remember exactly what you said, that Dad checked for a pulse, and she had none."

"You misunderstood me."

No, I hadn't.

# Chapter 40

A man was in jail for something he didn't do. My mother should have been in jail—again or still. And I was hiding stolen property in Aunt Birdie's attic.

During the weeks that followed my mother telling me the whole story, I did a lot of "what if" thinking. What if I let it all go—never again giving thought to the entire ordeal, went on with my life as if none of it had ever happened? What if I turned my mother in? What if I tried to sell the stolen property and live happily ever after? What if I turned it in anonymously? I didn't have any answers, and that kept me from deciding which way to go.

One day, not long after all this had come to light, I came home from school and joined my mom and aunt in the living room.

"We've been talking, Ben," Aunt Birdie said. "Your mother and I would like it very much if you told us your story, the whole story about the ordeal you went through after…well, you know, after she left."

My mother had been out of prison almost a year, so her wanting to hear the "whole story" now pissed me off. I felt my hackles rise and almost went off on my mom for waiting so long to show an interest, but I knew it was one of those "high roads" I was supposed to take.

"You know most of it," I told my aunt. "And you said you filled her in."

"Not all of it, and I think it would be good for your mom to hear it directly from you."

I glanced at my mom's face. No expression as usual. I suspected she didn't actually want to hear the story. It was probably Aunt Birdie who wanted her to hear it.

For the next two hours, I relayed the details of our scary ordeal. I told it exactly as it had happened, making no effort to spare my mother from any part that might induce guilt feelings in her. I did leave out two details. I couldn't bring myself to rat out Melvin. He had protected me, and I would continue to protect him. And I didn't want my mother to know I knew about the stash of stolen items I'd found in the room under her closet.

"You said you hid from the sheriff when he came," my mother said. "Where did you hide?"

"In the cellar."

"How'd you get in? We always kept that door locked."

Trapped. "Lucy showed me the secret room in your closet."

My mother struggled for words, her face pallid. "You went…you were down…did you. Weren't you scared?" she asked.

"Sure, we were scared."

"It's so dark down there."

"Tell me about it."

"We didn't keep much down there. It was such a small room."

"It was small alright."

"Did you…just stand up in there?"

"No, we sat on the floor."

"I see." She studied my face and waited for me to say something more, but I said nothing. I wanted her to squirm.

"So when you finally packed up things to take with you, how did you decide what to take?"

"I took whatever fit in the suitcase."

"I see."

"Here's something I'd like to know, Mom," I said, trying to change the subject. "How did the police know to come to our house after you left?"

She shook her head.

"I think I can fill in the blanks on that one," said Aunt Birdie. "When I came to in the hospital, I immediately told the nursing staff about your mom being in jail and that I was on my way to pick you up."

"How did you know Mom was in jail?"

"Her voice-mail message."

"Was Leah going to drive you?"

"No. I had leaned on her too much for rides everywhere, so I called for a cab to pick me up. And then I must have passed out on the front porch waiting for the cab. The cab driver found me. Anyway, when I told them about you and your sister, the nurses called your number and couldn't get through, so they called the police for them to check on you."

"They came more than once," I told her.

"I think your neighbor…I can't remember her name…may have also called someone, either the police or social services. I'm not sure."

"Mrs. Hornblower," I said.

"I think it's Hanover, Ben," my mother interjected. She had always called her Hornblower back then.

"And then they put out an Amber Alert on you two, and—"

"I didn't know that," Mom said. She stared at me. "Where were you when this happened?"

I couldn't tell her we were at Melvin's.

"I don't know. Either hiding from them or on our way here, I guess."

"You shouldn't have hidden from them," said my mother. "Anything could have happened."

*Look who's giving who advice on the right thing to do.*

"It's just awful that you and Lucy had to go through that, Ben," Aunt Birdie said. "And I feel like it was all my fault."

"It wasn't *your* fault, Aunt Birdie."

I told them how I took the Bronco and drove it as far as Casey's General Store in Galena and stuck to my usual story about how this Good Samaritan woman drove us to Aunt Birdie's. My aunt told my mother the rest of the story.

When all the details had been disclosed, Mom got up and retreated to her room.

"Maybe I should check on her," Aunt Birdie said.

"Let me. I have one more question to ask her," I said.

I expected the empty feeling in the pit of my stomach to flare up as I approached Mom's room. In the brief moment before I rapped on her door, while I thought of the right way to couch what I was about to ask her, I contemplated turning around and forgetting the whole thing, but something inside impelled me to move forward with it.

"Can I come in?" I asked her after tapping on the door.

"I'm tired, son. We can talk tomorrow."

"It's really important."

When she didn't respond for several seconds, I cracked open the door and peered in on her.

"C'mon in," she said through a sigh.

I sat down on the end of her bed.

"Something has been nagging at me for a while now," I told her.

"What's that?"

I conjured up the nerve to ask the question.

"Do Lucy and I have the same father?"

She turned her gaze from me to the window.

"Mom?"

She sat there without moving or blinking until she raised her hand as if to ward something off, perhaps my question.

"Well?"

She spoke without making eye contact.

"Whatever would make you ask such a question?"

"Just a hunch. Dad wasn't Lucy's father, was he?"

She shook her head.

"Who is, then?"

She shrugged.

"You don't know? How could you not know?"

"His name was Nick Slaughter."

"Who was he?"

"Just someone."

"Just someone?"

"Okay—someone I had an affair with."

"And Dad knew, didn't he?"

"Eventually."

"I remember the fight the two of you had over it. How did he find out?"

"He came home from work one night unexpectedly."

"Where was I? How old was I?"

"You were in bed. You must have been four or something."

"Wait a minute. Dad worked?"

She glanced up at me. "Your dad used to be a cop, Ben."

"What?"

"When he discovered us, well, it wasn't a pretty sight. Your father threatened to kill him."

"What happened to him?"

"After we were caught, Nick fled the area. I honestly don't know where he went. Never saw or spoke with him again. I soon put Nick behind us, but your dad didn't."

"What do you mean?"

"He said he was going to find him someday and kill the son-of-a-bitch."

"He wasn't mad at *you*?"

"Sure he was. I got my just desserts."

"Like what?"

"Not important."

"How long was this affair?"

"I don't know. Months."

"How many months?"

"Many."

"Why?"

"Why what?"

"Why'd you cheat on Dad?"

"Your father wasn't a very loving man. And I needed some. Nick gave me what your dad couldn't."

"And then Lucy was born."

"When I found out I was pregnant, I pretended it was your father's."

"How did he find out she wasn't his?"

"He confronted me on it one day. Said no kid of ours would come out with hair like that."

"We don't look much like brother and sister."

"Yeah, well, I guess your dad didn't think so either."

"So why did he stop being a cop?"

"He became obsessed with finding Nick, and it got in the way of his work. He was eventually canned because of it."

"Why?"

"He'd spend time trying to find this guy when he was supposed to be working on police matters. The more frustrated he got over it, the more he drank. The more he drank, the more he missed work. He got away with it for a while, but then one day he went out on an assignment drunk, fired his gun for no good reason, and almost hit a kid. Another cop witnessed it, and he was fired."

"Wow."

"After that he drank even more and treated me like shit. That never stopped."

"He was never mean to *us*."

"You didn't cheat on him."

* * *

My basketball coach had never called me into his office before—usually when one of us was in trouble, he'd make a public display of it—so when he did, I went there with much apprehension.

"Hey, coach, what's up?" I asked him with as much nonchalance as I could put on.

"Sit down, Ben."

"Am I in trouble?"

"You tell me."

"What do you mean?"

"You've been making stupid mistakes lately, letting me and your team down."

"Just having a bit of a bad run is all. I'll have my game back in no time."

"Your grades are borderline to remain on the team."

"Oh, that. I'll tell you, Mr. Jameson is the toughest grader I've ever—"

"Do you want to tell me what's going on?"

"Nothing, coach. I'm just in a slump, I guess."

"My experience tells me there's usually a reason for deteriorating grades."

"Nope. Nothing here."

"Is it a girl?"

"No. I'm not even going with anyone."

"Is it about someone you're no longer going with?"

"No. I'm over that."

"How are things at home?"

"Okay."

"You sure?"

"Yeah. Everything is good."

"Well, I don't want to pry. Just know that I'm here if you want to talk."

"Okay."

"And Ben?"

"Yeah."

"I'd hate to lose my star player. You've got to get those grades up."

"Yes, sir."

* * *

My mother and I never talked about Lucy's parentage after that initial discussion. There was no need to. My knowing it helped me to understand both my parents a little better, and for that I was grateful. But it also left me more conflicted over my feelings about my mom. She'd had an affair, which was wrong, of course, but then she had to deal with a husband who lost his job and turned to drinking because of it. That's why she'd worked six days a week in a job she hated—to support her family and maybe to get away from him.

After that discussion, Mom was still itching to know what I knew about the box of stolen items she'd stashed in our home but never came right out and asked me about it. She kept dropping little bombshells trying to get me to say something.

"Somewhere I heard that Mrs. Washington's gardener was charged with stealing items from her house," she told me. "Did you know that, Ben?"

"I read that he was charged with grand theft, but the charges were later dropped."

"I wonder what they thought he stole."

"Gee, Mom, I don't know."

She knew damn well he'd been falsely charged on both counts—theft and murder. And if she figured I knew where the stuff was and that she could possibly still profit from it, she was more screwed up than I'd thought.

That ate away at me—that my own mother had stolen from a helpless old lady, caused her death, and allowed an innocent man to go to prison for it. What kind of person does that? The more I dwelled on it, the more upset I became over it. Aunt Birdie must have sensed something was going on with me and confronted me one day in the car.

"Have you lost weight, Ben?" she asked me.

"I don't think so."

"It looks like it to me."

"Hmm."

"What's troubling you, dear?"

"Nothing."

"You can't fool me, Ben. I can see it on your face, in that clenched jaw you sport whenever you're around your mother."

"Naw. You're seeing things that aren't there."

"No, I'm not. What's bothering you about her? The fact that she's not back on her feet yet?"

"I don't think she'll ever be back on her feet—she's made no attempt at it whatsoever. Doesn't that bother you?"

"I think she would if she could. No one likes to depend on others for their existence."

"You sure about that? What's stopping her?"

"I think she's probably getting in her own way. Sometimes it's hard to break out of that routine."

"You know what I think she needs?"

"Probably, but tell me anyway."

"A good kick in the—"

"Okay, let's not go there."

"And you're helping her. If she didn't have you to lean on, she'd be forced to fend for herself."

"Maybe. Maybe not."

# Chapter 41

Two weeks before Thanksgiving, I felt I had to decide what to do about the stolen goods I was hiding. Melvin's advice to "do the right thing" and Mrs. Franzen's advice to "take the high road" ran through my head all too often.

But what if doing the right thing meant creating a destiny that was awful for someone? Including myself. Then what? Mom wasn't well. Could she even survive more prison? And I was just a kid. Did I deserve being punished for holding on to something she had stolen?

If I did the wrong thing—kept quiet—which had lesser consequences for my mother and me, it had the potential of haunting me for the rest of my life, like it was doing now.

I considered talking to someone about it. But who? I couldn't burden Aunt Birdie—she'd been through enough, thanks to my mother. Coach said I could talk to him about anything, but I knew what he'd say. He'd say, "Do the right thing." Come to think of it, no one would likely advise me to keep quiet about it—that would have to be something I'd decide on my own to do.

I could dispose of the stolen items—in a dumpster, a lake, a Salvation Army clothing drop-off box. But that didn't seem right. These things rightfully belonged to someone—whoever had inherited Mrs. Washington's estate when she died. That got me feeling even worse about the whole ordeal.

One day, I asked my mother about Mrs. Washington's relatives.

"She didn't have any relatives that I know of," Mom said. "None that ever came to visit her anyway."

"Was she ever married?" I asked.

"Nope."

"I wonder who she left her house to, all her stuff?"

"Probably that foundation of hers."

"What foundation is that?"

"I don't know the name of it."

"What does it do?"

She shrugged. "Something to do with kids."

Later that day, I Googled "Abigale Washington foundation" and learned that Mrs. Washington had had an autistic son who died in 1985. After he died, she formed the Leonard J. Washington Foundation that helped families with children who had autism, Down's syndrome, cerebral palsy, and various other developmental disabilities. According to the website, her foundation had helped more than five hundred families in twenty countries with financial and medical assistance.

I didn't have to think about it anymore. The what-ifs no longer mattered. I knew what I had to do.

* * *

Seventeen and scared to death, I sat on the end of a long, hard bench inside the drab walls of the Whiteside County Sheriff's Office, the weighty cardboard box of stolen items that I had guarded for the past five years planted on my lap. Turning the box over to the authorities was the right thing to do. While turning in my mother was also the right thing to do, it was a cross I knew I'd bear for the rest of my life. Both of our fates hung in the balance.

To pass the time while I waited, I reflected on the people in my life.

My family—Dad, Lucy, Aunt Birdie, and Mom. Dad, of course, was dead. After I heard Mom tell me about his past, I realized I didn't know him very well. Lucy was in a good place, but that didn't stop me from regretting that I didn't do more to protect her. My savior, Aunt Birdie, would…well, always be Aunt Birdie. And my mom…her fate was uncertain.

My best friend Will—I could only hope he was at peace and looking down on me every once in a while, being there for me like he always was, especially now.

Then there was Georgia, my first love. I often still thought about her.

I reflected too on Melvin, the man some would have called good-for-nothing, the man who could have been in big trouble if the authorities had found out that he had us in his possession during the Amber Alert, the man who stole from me, the man who helped me when I needed help the most.

With nothing better to do, I added up how long it had been since Lucy and I had been left alone to fend for ourselves on that fateful day—something I never could have done in my head without Will's tutoring. Nineteen hundred days. Exactly. Nineteen hundred to the day.

Nineteen hundred days of being scared, making tough decisions, and hating my parents for what they did to us. Nineteen hundred days with remnants of the past profoundly affecting me in one way or another. I looked forward to having that past lifted off my shoulders.

But even at that young age, I knew the past never really went away. It got finely woven into the present and the future—there to stay with you for every step of your life's journey, and who knows, maybe even beyond that. I could treat my past with contempt, resentment, shame, or embarrassment if I wanted. Consider it a burden and blame it for every bad choice I would make for the rest of my life. Or I could use it to my advantage—accept it, embrace it, and learn from it.

"Just do the right thing," he'd said.

While I waited, I thought about what kind of person I would have been if I hadn't had the life I had experienced so far. Right then, at three p.m. on a Sunday afternoon, I should have been home reminiscing about the previous night's date. But instead I was sitting in a sheriff's office getting ready to spill my guts about what I'd been hiding, poised to rat out my own mother. Ironically, I had her to thank for forcing me to grow up a little faster than normal—your average seventeen-year-old probably didn't have the guts to do what I was about to do.

Someone sat down beside me.

"Hey, kid," he said. "Thought maybe you could use a friend right about now, someone who knows a little too much about the judicial system."

I didn't know how he knew I was there and didn't ask. But there he was— a remnant of my past, a current advocate, and hopefully a future friend.

"Mr. Mattis?" the young woman in a too-tight sweater and gray-plaid skirt said to me. "The sheriff will see you now."

With the box of stolen items cradled in my arms and Melvin by my side, I rose from my seat and followed the young woman in the too-tight sweater and gray-plaid skirt to learn my destiny.

# Epilogue

"**A**re you worried about something, Daddy?"

"Why do you ask, sweetie?"

"I don't know. You just look worried."

I am worried—my mother coming to live with us wasn't an easy decision, and I am unsure how it will play out. "Maybe a little," I tell her.

"About what? Grandma Rose coming here?"

"Let's talk about that, Sadie."

Mom had fared better in prison than any of us had expected. Still, at fifty-two, with severe emphysema and other serious maladies, she couldn't be expected to live on her own. She had become remorseful while incarcerated—another surprise—telling me each time I visited her how bad she felt about all that had happened to Lucy and me because of her actions, including the three-year probation I received for my role in it. The judge had gone light on me since I hadn't taken possession of the items knowing they were stolen, and as soon as I figured it out, I took action. I suspect turning in my mother may also have been a factor in my sentencing. I was in college for most of the probation. The monthly visits with my probation officer and ten o'clock curfew didn't present much of a problem, but I never told her that.

"Grandma Rose is going to come live with us, honey."

Her eyes grow wide. "In our house?"

"Mm-hm."

"Where is she going to sleep?"

"In the spare bedroom."

"Next to mine?"

"Yes. Is that okay?"

"I guess so. What is she going to do all day?"

"I'm not sure. Her health isn't very good. But you'll be in school, remember?"

"Yep. Kindergarten," she says with pride.

"Here's something else you don't know. This used to be my Aunt Birdie's house before she died, and Grandma Rose and I lived with her. Before I went off to college, I used to sleep in your bedroom."

"You did? With fairies on the wallpaper?"

"Well, no. We put that up for you."

"Who's Aunt Birdie?"

"Aunt Birdie was my dad's sister."

"Your dad?"

"I had a dad when I was a kid, just like you have a dad."

"Where's your dad?"

"He's in heaven."

"What about Aunt Lucy?"

"What about her?" My sister Lucy is Sadie's only aunt, and they simply adore each other. Lucy—who is now a registered nurse, married, and trying to get pregnant—is a frequent visitor of ours, spending as much time with Sadie as she possibly can.

"Is she your aunt, too?" she asks.

"No, she's my sister."

"I'm all confused."

"I know, sweetie. It's complicated."

"When you all lived together, did they used to play basketball with you in the driveway?"

The basketball hoop Aunt Birdie had let me attach to her garage when I was a teenager still remains. I've tried more than once to get Sadie interested in shooting hoops with me, but she seems to be more interested in other things, like doing arts and crafts projects with her mother.

"No, they didn't. But I was good at it—helped me get into college."

"You were good at something?"

Gee, thanks a lot.

"Yes," I said, thinking back to that period of my life, "I was pretty darn good at basketball."

"Oh."

"That's what's in mommy's tummy, you know. A great big basketball."

"Don't be silly, Daddy. I know it's a baby. I even felt him kick."

"What makes you think it's a boy? We don't even know that. We want to be surprised, just like we were when you were born."

Sadie scrunches up that adorable little face of hers and shrugs.

"You remind me so much of your mother when you do that."

As if on cue, Georgia walks into the room.

"I just got off the phone with the doctor. I told her I *had* to know. So… she told me!" My pregnant wife is radiant as she smiles at me, and I savor the moment until I can't wait any longer.

"And?"

"It's a boy!"

I hope you enjoyed reading *Nineteen Hundred Days* and will consider posting a short review on Amazon and/or Goodreads. Reviews and word-of-mouth referrals play an important role in helping authors promote their books, and your help in this regard is much appreciated.

Do you belong to a book club? If you choose this or any other of my books, I'm happy to participate in your book club discussion. If you're local to northern Illinois or southern Wisconsin, I may be able to participate in person. If you are in some other part of the world, I can tune in by Skype or phone. Just shoot me an e-mail if you're interested—info@florenceosmund.com.

*Florence Osmund*

# Other Books by Florence Osmund

**They Called Me Margaret**

Cozy mystery writer Margaret Manning learns there can be a fine line between reality and fantasy when her husband's behavior mimics some of the shadier characters in her books.

*Told through the lens of main character, Margaret, this novel is jam-packed with many twists and turns (and unanswered questions) all tightly woven together to make it a real page-turner.*
—Barbara J. Dzikowski

**Living with Markus**

Forced to choose between cultivating a satisfying life for himself and rescuing his dysfunctional family members from their certain demise causes Marc to question the importance of family. Does he save his relatives from their ill-fated lives, or save himself from entering a life of self-sacrifice and missed opportunities? Painful soul-searching and late-night talks with the captivating tenant downstairs guide him to an unexpected decision and discovery of his true purpose in life.

*The characters, even the young boys, are complicated and believable, and the plot's complexity allows the reader to see the characters from a myriad of angles.*
—Windy City Reviews

**Regarding Anna**

After recovering from the shock of her parents' death, Grace Lindroth discovers clues in their attic that cause her to believe the two people she called Mom and Dad her whole life may not have been her real parents. In her search for answers, she encounters people whose actions cause her to be distrustful of just about everyone, heightening her determination to uncover the truth.

*For a fun, fascinating, and somewhat unpredictable mystery, look no further than Regarding Anna by Florence Osmund. Written in a friendly and straightforward style, readers will enjoy sleuthing alongside Grace as she seeks the truth about Anna. Don't be surprised if you have a hard time putting this novel down.*
—San Francisco Book Review

**Red Clover**

The troubled son of a callous father and socialite mother determines his own meaning of success after learning shocking family secrets that cause him to rethink who he is and where he's going. Lee Winekoop's reinvention of himself is surprising; the roadblocks he confronts are unnerving; and the cast of characters he befriends along the way is both heartwarming and amusing.

*Red Clover is a wonderfully written detailed story about a man overcoming his upbringing and becoming his own. The finished product, both the man and his story, are exemplary.*
—Windy City Reviews

**The Coach House**

1945 Chicago. Marie Marchetti flees from her devoted husband when she realizes he is immersed in local corruption, only to discover it's the identity of her real father that unexpectedly changes her life more than her husband ever could.

*This book is not only thought evoking but also a genuine pleasure to read.*
—BestChickLit

**Daughters** (sequel to The Coach House)
Discovering who her father is leads Marie Marchetti to discover who she really is and where she belongs, driving her to seek peace and truth in her life. But unexpectedly, the most life-altering consequence of her reunion grows out of an encounter with a twelve-year-old girl named Rachael.

*Civil rights, gender roles, and political postures are carefully, realistically, and sensitively present in this story.*
—Pens and Needles

Osmund's books are available on Amazon
http://www.amazon.com/author/florenceosmund

Or the author's website http://florenceosmund.com/buy_the_authors_books

Or at book stores who order from distributors Ingram or Baker & Taylor

# About the Author

After a long career working for large corporations, Florence Osmund retired to write novels. "I strive to create stories that contain thought-provoking plots and characters with depth and complexity, particularly ones that challenge readers to survey their own values," Osmund states.

Florence continues to write literary fiction from her home on a small, tranquil lake in a far north suburb of Chicago, where she lives with her 20-year-old feline companion Miska.

If you are a new or aspiring novelist, visit Florence's website where she offers substantial advice on how to begin the project, writing techniques, building an author platform, book promotion, and much more.

| | |
|---|---|
| E-mail | info@florenceosmund.com |
| Website | http://www.florenceosmund.com |
| Facebook | http://www.facebook.com/florenceosmundbooks |
| LinkedIn | http://www.linkedin.com/in/florenceosmund |
| Twitter | @FlorenceOsmund |
| Goodreads | http://www.goodreads.com/user/show/8800692-florence-osmund |
| Amazon | http://www.amazon.com/author/florenceosmund |

www.ingramcontent.com/pod-product-compliance
Lightning Source LLC
Chambersburg PA
CBHW070454120726
47910CB00003B/1045